TIMECOP

LARGO ENTERTAINMENT PRESENTS IN ASSOCIATION WITH JVC ENTERTAINMENT

A SIGNATURE/RENAISSANCE/DARK HORSE PRODUCTION A PETER HYAMS FILM

JEAN-CLAUDE VAN DAMME

"TIMECOP"

RON SILVER   MIA SARA

CO PRODUCERS TODD MOYER AND MARILYN VANCE   FILM EDITED BY STEVEN KEMPER

PRODUCTION DESIGNED BY PHILIP HARRISON   DIRECTOR OF PHOTOGRAPHY PETER HYAMS   EXECUTIVE PRODUCER MIKE RICHARDSON

BASED UPON THE COMIC SERIES CREATED BY MIKE RICHARDSON and MARK VERHEIDEN

STORY BY MIKE RICHARDSON & MARK VERHEIDEN   SCREENPLAY BY MARK VERHEIDEN

PRODUCED BY MOSHE DIAMANT AND SAM RAIMI AND ROBERT TAPERT

DIRECTED BY PETER HYAMS   A UNIVERSAL RELEASE

LARGO
ENTERTAINMENT
IN ASSOCIATION WITH JVC ENTERTAINMENT, INC   © 1994 LARGO ENTERTAINMENT

UNIVERSAL
AN MCA COMPANY

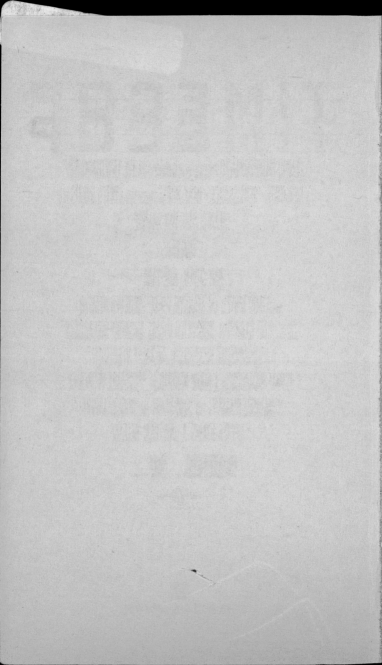

TIMECOP

A novel by S. D. Perry
Based on a screenplay by
Mark Verheiden
Story by Mike Richardson
& Mark Verheiden

BERKLEY BOOKS, NEW YORK

TIMECOP

A Berkley Book / published by arrangement with
MCA Publishing Rights, Inc.

PRINTING HISTORY
Berkley edition / September 1994

ISBN: 0-425-14652-9

BERKLEY®
Berkley Books are published by The Berkley Publishing Group,
200 Madison Avenue, New York, New York 10016.
BERKLEY and the "B" design
are trademarks belonging to Berkley Publishing Corporation.

PRINTED IN THE UNITED STATES OF AMERICA

10 9 8 7 6 5 4 3 2 1

"To every thing there is a season,
and a time to every purpose under the heaven."
—ECCLESIASTES 2:16

"Time is on my side."
—MICK JAGGER

Prologue

Gainesville, Georgia, 1863

When he first heard the dull splashing sounds of the approaching horses, he mistook it for more rain; it had been pouring buckets off and on all morning. His hat and clothes were soaked and it was still coming down, even though the thunder was now in the distance and the rain had eased off some. He cupped one hand around a cold and dripping ear, and managed to dump a brimful of chill water into his eyes with the move.

Jesus! He scowled and blinked it away. Goddamn weather.

Goddamn assignment.

After a moment, he made out the creaking of the wagon and the low murmur of conversation.

"Took you long enough," he said under his breath. His voice was easily covered by the rain, even slackened as it was now to a more gentle sound he was really starting to hate. All fucking morning he'd been crouched here in the downpour, had watched it trickle from the curved brim of his hat and off the ends of his dark, stringy hair until he thought he'd go crazy. There was nothing else to do in the middle of nowhere, hunched over in the thin brush next to a rutted, mucky trail on the grayest morning in the history of the world. Nothing to do but *wait*.

Time.

Well. He had plenty of *that*.

He straightened slowly, wincing at the stiffness in his legs. Tiny rivulets of water coursed down the folds in his long coat and splattered against his boot heels. He checked his weapons for the tenth time and then stepped out onto the muddy road.

Almost over, finally.

Another minute passed before the group rounded the bend in front of him.

They looked as gray as he felt, their tattered uniforms and scruffy faces blending into the heavy sky—four soldiers on horseback, rallied loosely around a beaten-up buckboard. Another Confederate sat on the wagon's splintery perch and shook the reins tiredly, urging the two sopping horses onward. The driver was in a trance; he didn't pull up until the team was almost on top of the waiting man.

He felt a smile twitch at the corner of his mouth. "Mornin'," he drawled. This part of it, at least, was going to be fun.

The soldier driving the wagon wore a casual face, but there was a trace of apprehension nestled there. The other soldiers sat up straighter in their saddles.

Good.

"Mornin'," the driver returned easily enough. "Y'all mind movin' aside?"

He stood and stared at the Confederate, feeling the adrenaline build. "You know what I think?" He licked at his wet lips.

"No, sir, I can't rightly say that I do."

"I think you got yourself a shipment of gold in that buckboard, gold that you're bringing to General Lee."

He watched, pleased, as all of their wary faces tightened and two of the horse riders shot alarmed glances at each other. They searched the bushes with quick looks, trying to see if he had accomplices. Their hands drifted toward their guns. Nobody was supposed to know about this, that was why such a small detail had been sent. The theory was, they'd sneak by a lot easier if they weren't noticed, if they seemed to be just another wagon of food being smuggled in.

Stupid hicks, they had no *idea* . . .

"Just who might you be?" The driver's voice was sharp now.

"Why, I'm a . . . friend of the Confederacy." The urge to grin was almost too much to resist as he watched the driver consider his answer. "More or less."

"Well, why don't y'all show just how good a friend you are . . . by steppin' aside."

He kept his face straight. "I'd be most happy to. Except first, I'd be much obliged if y'all would move away and give me that gold. See, I have a need for it. And you're gonna lose this war anyway; what's the point in throwing good money after bad?"

The soldiers looked at him, at one another, and at him again. One of the front horsemen scanned the bushes again, a puzzled frown on his gray face. No place to hide ambushers, he'd be thinking. This fool in the road must be crazy from the rain. He must be insane to try this, unless he had help.

No, it's just me, all by my lonesome.

Stupid *fuckin'* hicks.

"I don't believe I heard you correct," the driver said, his eyebrows raised.

"I think you did," he said. "I'd like you to give me that

3

gold now. I'll take it somewhere it'll do some good." He tilted his head slightly, sending a fresh torrent of rain from his brim. He gave them a little grin. Showed the artfully designed smile, complete with brown tobacco stains and a gap where his right eyetooth ought to be.

But his socks were wet and his feet were turning into fleshy prunes and he wanted to get on with it.

The driver frowned. "Listen, mister. It ain't very nice out here, as you can plainly see." He nodded randomly at the surroundings with his chin, not taking his eyes off of the stranger. "There are five of us. I don't know what you think you're up to, 'cept if you don't move *now,* I'd just as soon kill you as not."

One of the riders cracked an uneasy grin, and moved his hand to the flap of the holster covering his sidearm.

The driver went on. "You want to die in this miserable weather, that's your choice."

He couldn't contain it any longer, not in the face of such pathetic cockiness. It was unfair, knowing what was going to happen. Wet as it was, their guns probably wouldn't even go off. A huge smile spread across his face. "I'm askin' you one more time," he said. "You gonna give me the gold? Last chance. You can still just ride away."

The driver shrugged, his lips pursed, and reached for his rifle.

All of the riders went for their guns—

—and he jerked his coat open, pulled his weapons, and started firing.

He had Uzis, two of them, each with a thirty-round magazine full of 9mm. The Israelis designed their machinery to work in any kind of weather.

Work it did.

The horses shrieked and reared as the bullets smacked into the flesh of the soldiers. The burst of man-made thunder

4

was absurdly loud in the rainy afternoon, deafening. Blood sprayed across the mucky ground as the five men screamed, cut down, chopped apart by the automatic weapons' fire. Their final expressions of shock and fear were blown into bloody pieces along with the rest of their fragile bodies—their still-reaching hands, their ropy innards—all of it splattered to the soupy mud.

He held the triggers back until the submachine guns ran dry.

It was over too quickly for him, but after a few seconds there was nothing left to take down. Men, horses—they were all history.

He lowered the Uzis; thin tendrils of smoke wafted from the barrels and disappeared into the rain. He was dimly aware that he was still grinning, trickling drops of water running down his face, over his fake teeth. In front of him, spread out like some bizarre feast, lay the slaughtered men and animals. Shattered, steaming bodies poked up from the muck at odd angles. They'd never had a prayer. It was a bloodbath . . .

God, a bath! *I'd give my left nut for a hot bath right now* . . .

There was a thought. As he surveyed the lifeless scene, he felt a chill run up his aching spine, followed closely by a need to sneeze. He wiped his nose with the back of his hand, and his face was hot to the touch. Great. Just fuckin' *great,* a head cold from sitting in the goddamn rain. He'd better get a fat bonus for this one . . .

The skies opened up again; the rain renewed its onslaught as he stepped forward; the wind gusted and drove at him the heaviest cloudburst so far.

Figured. Jesus.

He spat in disgust and went to look at the gold.

One

Senate Oversight Committee Room,
Washington, D.C.,
September 2, 1994

McComb watched the older senator carefully, had watched him indirectly from the minute he stalked into the boardroom, five minutes later than everyone else. The man fascinated him. Harlan Utley, in spite of his rumpled suit and his consistent pretense of an inability to be punctual, was a powerful figure—he had been in the business for a long time, and he knew how to cover his ass . . . and how to get rid of his enemies.

All good things to know.

Of course, the young Senator McComb himself was no slouch—but he was still new here, and he knew he would do well to study with care men like Utley. The old man didn't fuck around, and he didn't wear the same air of skepticism that the others wore, tapping their pencils and raising their eyebrows as quiet seconds ticked by. Skeptical because the copied folders that lay in front of them were full of techno-garble that implied—well, what sounded like a joke.

McComb glanced at his watch—several thousands of dollars' worth of Swiss machinery, though it didn't look it—and allowed a flash of annoyance to cross his cultured features. He was going to miss part of the fund-raiser being thrown by OpticEx. He had a long ladder to climb before he had anything like Utley's clout, and he didn't like missed opportunities, not when it came to collecting fat corporate money. Money was what made the political world go around, and you could never have too much of it.

This meeting wouldn't have been called if it wasn't important, but Spota was keeping a room full of very busy people waiting, and from what McComb knew, Spota was too smart to piss off men like Utley unless he also had a very big hammer. That's how things worked in D.C. You either kicked ass or kissed it, depending on how much clout you had, and even a man with the President's ear had to pay attention to the rules or he'd be looking for a job real damned quick.

That's what it was really all about. Clout. Power. Whose nuts you had in your pocket and what you could make him do to get them back.

And speak of the devil . . .

George Spota, special assistant to the President, walked into the room and to the head of the long conference table. Right behind him was another man who looked familiar to McComb, although he couldn't quite place him. Obviously a nobody, with that hard-edged look that the young senator associated with cops and judges.

Did Spota need a bodyguard these days?

Spota arranged his lean body in his seat and raised his dark face to meet the waiting stares. The man was immaculate as usual, but there was something about his manner today that made him seem flustered. His eyes seemed particularly intense behind his rimless glasses.

McComb felt a stir on the back of his neck, an atavistic sense of danger. This was something big. Could it be that the information packet he had skimmed might possibly be *real* . . . ?

Spota started right in. "Good afternoon, gentlemen. The President is very grateful for your time here." His low voice was clear and deceptively amiable. "Believe me, this is a matter of the utmost importance—and, I cannot stress too much, the utmost secrecy."

"Why don't you cut to the chase, George?"

Everyone looked to McComb's end of the table, at Senator Utley.

"You're here to ask the committee for money, so why don't you just come out and ask for it." It wasn't a question. Utley didn't like to waste time either. "Then tell us why the hell you think there's a *prayer* you'll get it."

McComb and the others looked back at Spota, who smiled winningly. Like watching a finals match at Wimbledon. The up-and-coming young bull against the wily old stud. Even being this close was dangerous, and you sure didn't want to get between these two. You'd get gored and then stomped into the mud.

"Thank you for the advice, Senator. I *am* going to ask for money and there's no doubt in my mind you're going to give it to me."

A grin appeared on Utley's lined face. "We'll see about that, won't we, George?"

McComb felt that stir again, a warning from the small internal voice that had gotten him this far. Spota was sure of himself, no doubts. He had to be, because squeezing Utley for money was like squeezing a rock: How could he be so certain? He had to have a real big hammer.

McComb had a sudden feeling the OpticEx fund-raiser he was missing was going to be peanuts compared to what was going down here. He could *smell* it.

"Does the name Hans Kleindast mean anything to you?" Spota looked at each of the senators.

If anybody recognized the name, it didn't show. It rang no bells with McComb, and he knew anybody who was anybody in D.C.

"I didn't think so. He's a friend of ours, a physicist who just happened to have won the Nobel twenty years ago." He fixed his eyes on Utley. "And for the past few years, his field of research has been time travel."

Utley snorted. "Time travel." If Spota had said he'd brought back Jesus and was going to put on a demonstration of walking on water down in front of the Washington Monument, Utley's contempt and obvious disbelief couldn't have been any stronger.

"Time travel."

The senator glanced at McComb and the other senators, gave them a grin. "Well . . . beam me up, Scottie."

McComb grinned along with the others, including Spota. Utley could get away with the jab, just as he could get away with calling Spota George. McComb wouldn't have dared the joke or the first name. Not yet.

"That's very funny, Senator. You want to know what's even funnier than that?" Spota was still smiling.

Utley leaned over and gave McComb a stage-whisper aside: "I get the feeling he's going to tell us."

To Spota, he said, "Go ahead, George. Lay it on us."

Spota dropped the smile. "The funny thing is, the good doctor? Well, he actually did it."

McComb waited. The other senators shifted in their chairs, now wearing expressions that ran from mild amusement to open disbelief.

Utley didn't twitch. He was a master poker player. They said if he wanted to leave politics, he could go to Vegas or Atlantic City or the Mississippi casinos and make a fortune at the game. He knew a bluff when he heard one, and from his face, it seemed he didn't think Spota had the balls to try it on him.

Spota went on. "I thought that might get your attention." He gestured with one manicured hand at the table. "The technology is all in the folders in front of you, although you probably won't understand it any better than I can. It's got to do with the theory of relativity, and the effects of time as you approach the speed of light—" Spota half-shrugged. He was no scientist. "It all came from particle accelerators that were first built in the eighties. The idea is, you can go backward in time by going so fast you can arrive before you left—if you take a shortcut through hyperspace."

Spota paused for effect, which was unnecessary. McComb was riveted, the possibilities already starting to turn in his mind.

"You have to move in space, as well, so you don't wind up in the middle of something or the middle of nowhere—the Earth isn't in the same place it was yesterday or last year. But it can all be calculated with computers. You can pick a spot in time and a place, and within certain limitations you can put something or some*one* there. Apparently the reach is still somewhat limited, only a couple of hundred years. So, no dinosaur hunts or visits to Golgotha.

"Of course, as you might suspect, it gets real tricky, time travel. Things like the Grandfather Paradox. If you go back in time and change something . . . it's serious. It could be catastrophic. It's like throwing a stone in a pond, and it causes ripples in the water—only it's ripples in time, and they can be disastrous. If someone wanted to go back and . . . kill Hitler, say, which would seem like an appropriate use for such a device—it might cause a chain reaction of events that could alter—even destroy—mankind."

Spota leaned forward, his dark features grim. "This sounds like science fiction, but trust me, it is all *real*."

From a million miles away, McComb heard Utley speak. "That's some pretty farfetched stuff we're talking about here, George. And real big."

Spota nodded. "Couldn't be bigger. The problem is, gentlemen—the cat is already out of the bag. The technology is there. Our pal Kleindast may not be the only one who has figured this out. There are others working along the same lines. And that is where you, my good senators, come in."

He glanced at the man who had accompanied him into the meeting and then continued. The short, dark-haired stranger raised his chin slightly; he hadn't spoken a word yet, but his part was apparently coming up.

"If you will give me for a moment that this technology works, then you will also see that the government of the United States will as a result have a major responsibility, gentlemen."

McComb didn't see what he was driving at, but Utley did. He was a sharp old blade. "Control," he said.

"Exactly. The cat *is* out of the bag. We can't have it jumping into the pond making waves, now can we? We need a watchdog. To make sure it goes where we want and doesn't do what we *don't* want."

Utley nodded. He saw something the rest of them didn't see. He had a mind sharp as a truckload full of razor blades.

McComb was no slouch in the thinking department, either. He thought about it for a second, and it dawned on him what it was.

Holy shit—

"Time Cops," Spota said. "We had to form a new agency to police this technology. To actually *protect* time from those who would alter it."

12

McComb nodded. It made sense.

"We are proposing an agency that we will call the Time Enforcement Commission, the TEC. This man seated next to me is Commander Eugene Matuzak, of the D.C. Police Department; he is the President's choice to run the organization."

McComb allowed himself a flash of pride as Matuzak nodded politely to the senators. A cop, bingo.

Utley cleared his throat. "How much is this going to cost?"

Spota met his gaze. "A lot."

"How much is a lot?"

"More than a little and less than too much."

McComb knew it was unlike Spota to be so coy. He probably knew to the dime how much he wanted. This was going to be spendy. McComb waited silently with the others, not letting his impatience show. He wouldn't speak until it was necessary—but he wanted to see this project get funded.

Spota continued with the pitch. "Look, once people know how to do something, all it takes is money."

McComb nodded inwardly. Money was all . . .

Utley frowned. "This is not the best time for this. The economy is in crappy shape—"

Spota interrupted. "Excuse me, Senator, but whatever it costs will be cheap, given what might happen. You're too smart to believe otherwise. Suppose one of our foreign competitors goes back in time and invents the computer— or the airplane, or the automobile? You want to talk about the state of the economy? How about this one: Saddam Hussein finances a trip back to 1944 and Iraq becomes the first country to have the atomic bomb."

The room went deathly still.

"You like that one?" Spota said. "I can think of worse. Given a minute, you all can too."

Utley's face was set, not revealing what was on his mind. But Spota had to know he'd hit a sore spot with the old Senator. Utley had wanted to bomb Iraq back to the Stone Age during the Gulf War and he still wanted to have the CIA bump Hussein off.

"It's an interesting problem," Utley said.

McComb watched the Special Assistant intently. What he said next would either cinch the deal or blow it, and McComb suddenly wanted it cinched tight. In fact, he had never wanted anything so badly. The possibilities bloomed like desert flowers after a rain. Time travel. A smart man could control the world, if he could control the past.

Talk hard, Spota.

"Try this one on for size. We think there's already been a ripple. Ten days ago, the CIA broke up an arms sale to a bunch of middle-eastern terrorists in Hamburg. That's happened before, and ordinarily that kind of news doesn't occupy much of the President's desk. What made this one different is the fact that the arms were purchased with gold bullion . . . and the gold bullion was marked with the date 1863, stamped 'Property of the Confederate States of America.' It appeared to have been freshly minted."

"So what? You got yourself a Civil War buff, what does that prove?" Utley said. "Guy pours some gold into a mold, he can mark it any way he wants, can't he?"

"Or if they have the technology, they can go back in time and collect it," somebody at the other end of the table said. McComb wasn't paying attention, he didn't catch who it was who spoke.

Utley said, "If that's what they did. Maybe they just dug the stuff up and polished it. Gold doesn't go bad, now does

14

it? That would be a lot easier to believe than what you're selling, George."

Spota dropped the other shoe. "They did some sophisticated tests, Senator. I can't begin to tell you what they were, but the bottom line is, the gold was genuine Confederate bullion, produced *exactly* the same way as it was made more than a hundred thirty years ago, the way we measure time, but cast into ingots less than a year back. No mistake. That's a major contradiction. No way to explain it—except one."

"You're sure?"

"We have the smartest, the best minds in the world looking at it. We're sure. Somebody went back there and collected it."

McComb looked at Utley. Watched the older man's face, could almost see his mind churning behind it.

"Our committee would have exclusive jurisdiction over this project?"

Yes! He was going to go for it!

Spota's gaze bored into the senior Senator. "Yours and yours alone. No one can know about this, it's too dangerous. Look—*some*body is going to get control of this."

The rest of it didn't need saying. Us or them—whoever *they* were these days.

Utley nodded. "All right, George. I hope to hell this isn't like that bullshit Star Wars program, but if you can put it down in top secret black and white so I can show it around to the right people, I think you'll probably get your money."

He didn't even ask how much.

Utley looked around the table, studying each of the members' faces.

McComb was ready.

"Who wants to subchair the oversight on this sucker?"

Trick question. If this was some kind of science fiction fairy story, being involved with it could be major ammunition for an opponent come next reelection campaign: *Ladies and gentlemen, the incumbent senator believes in time travel. I wonder, does he also believe in Santa Claus, the Tooth Fairy and the Easter Bunny? Little bitty green men from Mars . . . ?*

Jesus, it would be worse than getting caught in bed with a trio of hookers. But if it *was* real . . .

McComb tilted his head slightly, never taking his eyes off of Spota. "I'd like to take a crack at it," he said casually.

"Ah, young Senator McComb. Yes . . . why not?" Utley smiled at Spota. "Oh, you'll like him, George. He's very much like you, except his dorsal fin is a little bigger."

McComb finally grinned as he stared down at the file of papers in front of him. Coming from Utley, that meant a lot. And these men didn't know it yet, but if this was legit, they had just handed him a golden key card to the fucking *world*.

He could smile at that.

Yessir . . .

Two

Max Walker was exactly one minute early when he spotted the most beautiful woman he had ever seen. He was sure of the time because her face was reflected in the window of a clock shop—ironic, really, after the morning he'd had, that he would see this gorgeous image overlaid by time passing. The ticking could be heard from his vantage point, several meters away, even in the semi-crowded D.C. strip mall where brightly dressed shoppers talked and laughed loudly. The acme of civilization, the mall—if you were fourteen.

What a woman. Her smooth, creamy features, her dreamy clear eyes, her full mouth—even as a translucent copy, she was breathtaking.

The seconds passed too quickly; he could have watched her for hours. But as he gazed on, lost in the memories of other times, the clocks in the window clicked to noon and began to chime. Dull, buzzing alarms, cuckoos, regal gongs. Passersby stopped to listen. Some of them saw the woman and smiled.

He moved toward her.

Walker watched her eyes brighten as he came up behind her, and something in his chest melted a little.

"There's never enough time, is there?" he said softly.

She didn't turn around, just studied his face in the window. "Never enough for what?"

Walker smiled slowly. "Women. One in particular, say."

"Then you never want to miss an opportunity," she said. Her perfect lips curved upward slightly.

He could smell the perfume she wore, something light and spicy. Maybe it was her hair . . .

"Are you busy?"

"I'm meeting my husband."

"If I were him, I wouldn't keep you waiting." He wanted to bury his face in that hair, inhale her softness and beauty.

She rustled her packages and raised one eyebrow playfully. "Tell you what—if he isn't here when I turn around, I'll go home with you."

"Such a deal!" Walker's heart thumped loudly as she turned to face him. God, she was something! One look from her and he was a fumbling adolescent again, struggling to keep from blushing—and to keep his pants in order . . .

"You'll do," she said, and put her arms around him.

His own came up to encircle her, and her eyes flickered closed. He bent down and touched her lips with his, heart still pounding. If he accomplished nothing else in his life, that was okay—as long as she would stay with him forever . . .

Melissa Walker stepped back and smiled. "I didn't hear you leave this morning, Mr. Walker."

He shrugged, relishing the lingering taste of her kiss. "It was early. I was meeting Matuzak."

A slight crease furrowed her smooth brow. "You're going to take that damned new job, aren't you?"

He'd been trying for several hours to think of a way to tell her, a way that wouldn't sound like a trite rationalization or a macho-bullshit excuse. Walker opened his mouth—

—and closed it again.

Noise washed over him, intruding on his thought.

He looked over at the mob of moving shoppers and spotted the kid, a young punk on in-line skates, carrying a radio on one scrawny shoulder, raucous music blaring. The heavy bass vibrated Walker's bones. Rap music, if that wasn't a contradiction in terms. Who was it making that racket? Somebody Dog Doo? If that wasn't the name, it should be. Maybe you had to be teenaged or black or both to appreciate it. He was neither.

Melissa started to pull him away, to go someplace quieter, probably, but Walker kept watching the guy with the boom box.

The kid had a seedy look to him; he wasn't a golden child. And he circled closer and closer to a little old lady with an obviously stuffed purse. The woman was alone and rather frail-looking. The kid spiraled in for the kill . . .

"Wait here," said Walker, his gaze never straying from the punk kid and the elderly woman, who still hadn't noticed that she was being edged in on.

Melissa sighed. "More hours, more risk, same pay. Can't pass that up, eh, hon?"

"Hold that thought. Be right back," he said.

He was only a step or two away from Skates when the kid snatched the woman's purse and backed one heel up to speed off with it.

Walker didn't even think. He hooked one arm out around the kid's and spun him away.

The kid's back slammed into one of the storefront windows, hard but not quite enough to break the glass. He still clutched the bag. The radio fell, smashed into pieces, and shut up.

Worth it for that alone. Without pausing, Walker twisted and fired a spin kick, up and around—

He stopped the bottom of his foot an inch away from impact with the surprised punk's grimy face.

He held his foot suspended there. As if it were carved from oak. As if he could stand here with his leg in the air all day, a living statue. Control, that was what fighting was all about. If you could control yourself, you could control others.

The kid started to shake.

"Read it," Walker said.

Skates leaned back as far as the window would allow, searched the bottom of Walker's shoe, desperate to comply.

"Uh . . . Wolverine . . . ?"

Walker let his boot move a centimeter closer. "*Between* the lines," he said.

The kid blinked several times, and dull comprehension spread across his sweaty brow. "Uhh . . . I—I, uh, should . . . get the fuck out of here . . . ?"

"Brilliant." Walker lowered his leg slowly and rested it on the tiled floor. He and Skates both glanced at the handbag.

"That purse doesn't go with your outfit," said Walker.

The kid kept his face carefully neutral as he skated over to where the old woman stood, an expression of amazement across her wrinkled features. He handed her the bag without a word, then turned and skated away fast, taking long strides. He got at least halfway down the strip before turning to flip Walker off, and then he disappeared into the crowd.

Walker briefly considered running after him, but Melissa was waiting. Besides, he'd never catch the punk. They could fly on those in-line wheels. He'd seen a shoplifter outrun two uniforms on bikes, once. They gained on him on the straights, but the thief did some tricky turns and lost them. No way he was going to sprint through a crowded mall just to smack a kid who'd given him the finger. It was graveyard bravado anyhow. The kid had been so scared of Walker he'd almost puked.

Walker turned back toward his wife and walked through the small mob of shoppers who had stopped to watch. They smiled and muttered to one another, and a few people even clapped. Everybody liked to see the triumph of good over evil—as long as they didn't have to get personally involved, of course.

He noticed a pair of onlookers who stood near the back, because they weren't smiling, just watching his face with grim intensity. Two men, rough-looking, both of them wearing long coats. When they saw his gaze, they each immediately dropped their own and then started to drift along with the dispersing crowd.

Walker followed them for a moment with his stare and then let it go. D.C. had all kinds. Couldn't bust a man for looking suspicious; you did that, you'd have to put away half of Congress and most of the Senate . . .

He walked back to where Melissa stood patiently waiting.

"Smart kid," he said, smiling. "He read my mind."

Melissa rolled her eyes. "With your English, he didn't have much of a choice," she said sweetly.

Walker raised his eyebrows a few times. "I know all the good words," he said, and then whispered a few into one of her exquisite ears.

Melissa laughed, a chiming sound more melodic than any other—with a trace of seductiveness underlying the tone. It had been that laugh that had drawn him to her so long ago . . .

They started walking together down the strip, her shoulder warm against his arm.

After a few steps, Melissa glanced at him. "You never

answered my question. You're going to take that new job, aren't you?"

Walker hesitated a second and then nodded. He didn't want to try to con her; their marriage was too good for that, and they had gotten this far by keeping the bullshit level to a minimum.

"I think so."

She sighed. "This new thing, this TEC, it's going to be dangerous, isn't it?"

They had been through this before, and he knew she understood as best she could. "I don't bake cookies for a living, 'Lis."

She acknowledged that with a tilt of her head and paused, lips pressed thoughtfully together. "Will you have to travel?"

Walker smiled. "In a manner of speaking. Not like you think."

His wife arched one of her fine brows upward, and seemed about to say something else, when a bright, strobing light washed across her features.

They both turned and looked at the smiling man with the Polaroid. He held a developing photograph out in their direction, "$3.00" stenciled neatly across a card in his hatband.

"Pictures bring back your memories," he said, still grinning. "Freezes time forever. When you're old and gray, you remember this day."

It was memorized patter and Walker smiled, ready to move past.

Melissa reached for the picture and held it a moment. She smiled at Walker.

"You're going to be very happy you got this," she said.

Walker took out his wallet and handed the man three

dollars. The guy tipped his hat to the two of them and walked happily on.

"What makes you think so?"

Melissa stared at the photograph. "I can see into the future," she said. Her voice was quiet and half-serious.

Walker peered at her closely. "What do you see?"

Melissa shook her head slightly and then ran one finger delicately around the edge of the picture. "I think it's going to rain this afternoon," she said.

The skies had been clear all morning. He almost laughed, but was caught by the hint in her voice.

"We both have the afternoon off," she continued, walking on. He realized that they were headed toward one of the mall's exits. "So I am *sure* it is going to rain. We'll have to stay inside, or we'll get wet."

She looked into his eyes then, and all thoughts of the punk kid and the TEC fell away.

"Of course, if we stay inside, we still might get wet. So, given that, why don't you see if you can walk the walk as well as you talk the talk, eh, Walker?"

He grinned. He had been hoping that she might say something along those lines. He held the door open for her as they stepped together out into the sunny parking lot.

As always, it was magic to be with her. He hoped it would last forever.

Three

Dusk drifted through their room, accompanied by the soft thumps of rain pelting the panes of glass in the gentle gray light. Walker sat cross-legged in bed while 'Lissa stroked his back with her long fingers. He grinned, musing at the rain; apparently she *could* see into the future, just a little bit.

It had been good, as it usually was—and there had been an intensity to their lovemaking today that would have frightened him once, an intimacy of spirit that he had come to cherish. As a younger man, he would have run from it, scared of what it implied. And yet each time with her, it seemed to get better. Deeper. He didn't see how it could get much better and leave him able to move. Or even breathe . . .

Melissa started rubbing his neck, and he rolled his tousled head to one side. She slid one hand down over his shoulder blades and across his thigh, to circle his groin. He arched his back. Moaned a little.

Melissa curved her body around his and lowered her head to caress him with her mouth. Walker took a deep breath and lay back across the rumpled sheets as she suckled at him.

After a few moments, she worked her way up his tightened abdomen with her tongue and teeth, nipping at him lightly, her long, smooth legs pressed against his. The feeling of her breasts nestled against his belly was both sweet and exciting; he wanted to take her in his arms and love her, be inside of her again . . . .

Melissa straddled his hips and he slipped into her. She dropped her head down, her silken hair brushing across his skin. He pulled her down, closer, her tongue flickering into the corners of his mouth, her hands buried in his hair as she rode him smoothly.

Her breath quickened, accompanied by the soft moans that meant she was getting closer. He began to thrust harder, his hands resting against her moving hips, and she leaned back, hair across her lips and eyes.

Walker gritted his teeth and slipped into a steady rhythm, feeling her all over his body. After a moment, she cried out and collapsed across him, whispering his name and biting at his lips. He pushed into her, all restraint gone now, and released his aching pleasure into her softness.

They lay there for an indefinite time, languishing. Twilight shadows crept across the floor as he stroked her back absently, wondering how he'd gotten so lucky. They didn't always see eye to eye, but they had found ways to make it work; he couldn't imagine life without her . . .

Finally, she stirred, rolled over to curl up beside him. They studied each other, Walker running his fingertips across her perfect features. The day of their wedding, he had known he could never tire of looking at her.

"Max . . . ?" Her brilliant eyes sparkled.

"Mmm?"

"There's something I want to tell you." She took a deep breath, smiling, and then laughed at her own pronouncement.

"What's that?"

She stopped laughing, but the smile remained. "Well, it's . . . Hmm, how can I put this . . . ?"

The phone trilled from the bedside table.

"Well, shit." He rolled his eyes and she stopped smiling as he reached toward the blaring instrument.

She touched his arm, a pleading look on her face.

"Breaks the mood, all right. I'm sorry," he said.

"Don't answer it, Max," she said.

For a second, he pulled his hand back. It *was* his afternoon off—wasn't it? But they wouldn't call if it wasn't necessary—

"I have to," he said.

The phone continued to ring.

"This one time, this *one* time . . ." Her face started to cloud up like the skies outside.

Dammit, this was not going to be some kind of a test, she *knew* how important his job was to him. He would like nothing better than to lock himself away with her, away from the outside world—but his life was more than that, and so was hers.

"I'm sorry," he said again, and picked up the phone. "Walker."

He looked at his wife as he listened to the voice on the other end of the line.

"Now? Christ, can't you find somebody else?"

She was up and out of the bed, grabbing angrily for her robe.

Walker scowled into the phone. Watched her sweep out of the bedroom on a wind of rage. Said: "I'm on the way," and slammed the receiver down.

Fuck.

And it *was* raining.

• • •

It was fully dark by the time he got out of the shower and into his uniform. Melissa wasn't in the bedroom, and he knew by the silence that she was waiting downstairs.

He tucked in his shirt, nearly tripped as he went down the stairs and toward the living room. He opened the front closet door and then stopped at a flicker of movement in the front room behind him.

She sat on the couch, half behind him, her legs folded beneath her and her arms crossed. The room had been straightened, their magazines stacked and set aside, the coffee mugs taken into the kitchen. She was always very neat. She got even neater when she was pissed off. They both did. The one benefit of arguing—the house always looked better when they kissed and made up.

He turned back to the closet. "Look, I'm sorry. Somebody called in sick, and—" He paused, searching.

"And there was no one but Max Walker to keep the streets safe, to clean up this town, to get all the bad guys. No one." Her voice rose, threatening tears.

He felt his shoulders drop. "I said I was sorry," he said. "It's not like I have a choice . . ."

"Of *course* you have a choice!"

"This is what I do," he started, feeling a stir of anger. Hadn't they settled this a long time ago? "I'm on call twenty-four hours a day; you knew that when we got married."

"I know," she said, almost dismissively, and he realized that wasn't the issue—at least not all of it. "It's just that now things are . . . different."

"What are you talking about?" he said. He tried to make it come out gently.

"This is not the way I wanted to do this," she said. He waited, but she didn't say anything else. Seconds passed.

"Look," he said finally, "I'm sorry. I have to go." He reached into the closet and pulled out his gun belt, then strapped it on. The new Glock was lighter, but he didn't like it as much as his old piece. A Tupperware gun, some of the guys called it. At least it was a decent caliber, a .45 and not a pussy 9mm.

He turned and went to her, and saw that tears had run tracks down her face. Her lips, still swollen a little from their afternoon, quivered.

Dammit.

Walker touched her mouth with one finger. "I won't be long. Just a few hours. There was something you wanted to tell me?"

"Yes."

"Can it wait till I get back?"

She nodded once, looking up at him. She attempted a smile, and he was proud of her for trying. They would work this out. He would make it up to her when he got back. Take her out for a late dinner, maybe, a trip to that bookstore she liked. Something. Every couple had a few bumps in their marriage, right? They'd get past this, just as they had every time before.

"Sure."

He kissed her and walked to the front door. He opened it and nodded at her, reaching to pull his collar up against the brisk wind. "I'll be home soon as I can," he said, hoping he could keep that promise.

He stepped outside—

—and his head shattered. Red and purple flared, turned to darkness, swallowed him as he fell to his knees with the shock of the impact. Something big, heavy—

"Surprise," said someone. A man's voice.

Walker fought to make him out, could only see the

bottom edge of a long coat and blood dripping from the butt of a shotgun—

Blood . . .

He shot his arm out to take down the man who had made him bleed—

—and he saw his own hand as it flailed weakly toward the pants leg, a million miles away—

Melissa screamed, and Walker tried to find her. Behind him—

"Max!"

She slammed the door. Tried to—

Good girl, smart—

But something stopped her. Shotgun. Walker rolled his head to see and fell to the pavement. Shotgun pawed at his wife, jerked her. She fell back against him, her face angry and full of pain—

—*for me—*

—and the hard wind slammed the door solidly closed. The sound was the loudest thing Walker had ever heard.

He was groping to turn around, to get to Shotgun, when another man appeared in front of him, and then the muddy shoes of a third. Long coats—

Long coats—where—?

Another explosion on top of the last. Pain—intense, sharp—and he struggled to stay awake as his eyes filled with red—

—The butt of another shotgun caught his chin, flipped him onto the soaking lawn. Rain and wind crashed around his head. He tried blindly to get his feet under him. The dark, wet grass came into focus—

—and spun away as he was gripped by iron claws. He looked up into the face of a giant, an ugly man.

The third man, behind him, held another shotgun. So much hardware.

Through the veil of blood in his eyes, he recognized two of them:

From the mall, the men from the mall—

The huge man clutching him unleashed a series of snap-kicks into Walker's gut. He tensed, but he already couldn't breathe.

He was jerked to an upright position, and he battled to get his legs to work, to block—

The giant's fist smashed into his face. The giant laughed. Enjoyed feeding him pain.

Walker shook his head, felt more than saw his blood fly into the rain.

Too much. He and the ground collided.

The other man, back at the step, called out. "All right, come on! He wants him in the house!"

Walker couldn't move, couldn't, until another sound mixed with the rain. High, angry sounds. Frightened.

From the house, screaming!

Melissa—

He pushed the ground away from himself, hurting too much to move, somehow got to his knees.

"Melissa!"

The big man's leg came up and smacked into Walker's bloody nose. Walker crashed forward again while Melissa screamed. He tried to crawl toward the house, dug into the dirt with hooked fingers. Had to . . . get to . . . her . . .

From above him, he heard deep, nasty laughter. A voice: "Tough bastard, ain't he?"

His legs went dead as a boot dug into his spine.

"Finish him!" the man with the shotgun yelled.

Melissa had stopped screaming. Walker wanted to close his eyes and let it be done, but Melissa could be hurt—

Why had these men done this thing, why were they killing him? Where was she?

He opened his mouth and felt blood trickle from one corner. He breathed into the mud, his voice invisible in the rain.

". . . Who are you?"

Walker looked up and prayed that this man would answer all of his questions, would let him get to Melissa.

The giant drew a .45 out from his coat; it glittered blackly in the light from the house. He pointed it at Walker's chest. The muzzle was huge; he could have stuck his fist into it.

"You're a smart boy," the man said, and his finger tightened on the trigger. Walker saw the finger move . . .

—No—!

The muzzle exploded with light and a boom, and in the sudden darkness that swam over him, he heard the faintest whispers.

". . . *why don't you sleep on it?*"

The rain.

Dying?

"Let's move! We gotta get out of here!"

Walker couldn't breathe. He choked, the air solid, the pain unbearable, and vomited into the mud in which he lay facedown.

He rolled over, still retching, and clawed at his broken chest. The vest. Had he—did he . . . ?

Yes.

He wasn't dead, not yet. Thank God, thank—

"Max!"

Walker stumbled to his feet and looked up. Her anguished face, pale and terrified, was pressed to their bedroom window. She started to sob, and he found the strength to move. He would go inside, go up, get her. She was alive. Everything else was unimportant.

He made it to the front door, but it was locked. He fumbled for the keys, but they were somewhere else, so he began to beat at the wooden frame with his fists. His feet slipped in the bloody muck beneath his shoes.

He backed away and then threw himself at the door. There was a crack, but it was solid. He moved back again.

"Melissa!"

The door gave way—but it flew *out*ward, knocked him flying back out onto the lawn.

As his house exploded into flames and thunder.

A thick shard of glass ran across his temple, cutting deep, but he didn't really feel it. He didn't feel any of it suddenly—the wounds, the freezing water all around, the broken ribs—

'Lissa!

He tried to sit up, couldn't manage it, had to settle for turning toward the house.

Flame spewed like dragon's breath from the devastated walls of the room where she had been, the colors of firelight dancing on the broken window glass, black smoke boiling out into the rain.

He didn't, *couldn't,* comprehend it, any of it, it wasn't reality—

Tears welled up in his eyes and spilled salt into his wounds.

He was still crying when it all went to black . . .

Four

Wall Street, October 30, 1929

Walker stepped into Atwood's private office exactly four minutes before Atwood was going to come in. He locked the double doors and looked around.

It was a nice room, big, wood paneling, carpet; a trio of slender, fluted metal deco torch lamps stood against one wall. There were padded leather chairs and a heavy oak coffee table set to one side, and the whole place smelled faintly of expensive cigars. A man's room, dedicated to the business of men. In this period, women only rarely figured into high finance.

He pulled his pistol and walked to the desk, weapon ready; he hoped he wouldn't have to use it. He'd brought an HK—the plastic Glock didn't travel well, they'd learned, though nobody knew why, exactly.

He was alone, on the tenth floor of the Floatbauer and Truesdale Brokerage Concern, in a room just next to the communal main office. It sounded frantic out there, not a surprise when you considered the date. There was an old-fashioned Philco console radio behind the desk. Walker reached over and flipped it on. It took a second for anything to happen as the tubes warmed up. A blast of loud static came finally. He turned the volume down.

A voice syrupy enough to cause diabetes said, ". . . and that was the mellifluous voice of Cray McDonough and his Irish—"

Walker turned it off. Some hit parade. They were a long way from retroZulu rock here.

There was a distant scream from down in the street, joined by a chorus of other shouts. Followed by a sudden, final crash that Walker heard even over the commotion outside the office.

Walker moved to the window and looked out through the wooden slat blinds in time to see a mob of onlookers push forward to the base of the building he was in. He noticed that most of the men wore hats, all of the women were clad in dresses or blouses and skirts. Almost immediately, two mounted policemen reined up and started to clear the crowd. Apparently the jumper had landed on a parked car.

He glanced at his watch and nodded to himself; that would be Floatbauer . . . The man had died right on the schedule. Amazing that men would jump off tall buildings and kill themselves over money. Alive, you could try again; dead was dead forever, no chance to change anything, no hope at all. Suicide was stupid, right up there with war.

The doors rattled briefly as one of the secretaries or another colleague tried to get to a window. It sounded yet more chaotic on the main floor, men and women crying and shouting. Walker touched the long-healed scar that twisted down his temple, the gesture almost absent. His own personal reminder of death.

Time was short, so to speak. He raised his weapon and went to stand beside the door.

A minute passed. He heard the siren of a 1920s ambulance out in the street.

He waited.

The door rattled again, this time with the metallic click of keys against tumblers. And in walked Lyle Atwood, clutching his briefcase and the day's paper. Walker could see "Market Crashes" in 60-point letters across the top of the newspaper.

The phone started to ring the second Atwood walked in. He slammed the door behind him and walked to the desk, set his briefcase down. He hooked the receiver under his chin and unlatched the case, stood there, his back to Walker.

"Yeah. Yeah. Let me talk to Ross."

Atwood pulled another newspaper from his case as he waited for Ross. Walker could only make out the top headline, "L.A. Smog Kills Forty." He had read it earlier, a current *USA Today*—July 12, 2004.

Walker watched as Atwood opened each newspaper to its financial section and lay them across his desk. Greed didn't suit him. He had put on a small belly, and there was a slickness to his features that hadn't been there before. He had lost more hair, too. Sad. Though that was the least of it.

"Ross! I want another ten thousand AT&T. Yes, I know— call it an act of faith. I really think things are going to turn around. Right, I got a crystal ball, I can see into the future. Yeah. Yeah."

He hung up and started to round the desk toward his wooden chair, grinning.

No time like the present . . .

Walker stepped out from the shadows and aimed his weapon at Atwood, who turned, warned somehow. Saw a gun pointed directly between his shocked eyes.

Atwood collapsed into his chair, grin wiped away. A flurry of expressions fled across his face—surprise, recognition, dread. All replaced by a pleading look that Walker didn't like, had never thought he would see.

37

Shit. He hated this more than he'd expected, now that he was into it.

"Walker . . ."

He moved closer, gun never wavering. "So how are you, Lyle?"

Atwood raised his hands slowly, and Walker wondered what one of the passing secretaries might think if they could see into the office—a man in a shiny, buckled TEC uniform, not a twenties outfit by any means, pointing a funny-looking gun at Mr. Atwood. Probably not *too* bizarre around here these days—according to the files, the crash sent a lot of people over the edge.

Atwood was no poker player; a nervous, cheesy grin appeared on his face, and his palms opened outward. "Hey, partner," he said, with a tone of voice that suggested he was happy to see him. Sad.

"Ex-partner," said Walker. "Are you armed?"

Atwood shook his head earnestly. "No. I'm a business-man. This is Wall Street. It wouldn't be appropriate."

Walker sighed and holstered his weapon. Whatever else he might have become, Atwood hadn't ever been a liar. Walker moved closer to the desk and snatched up the *USA Today*. He flicked a glance at the briefcase; inside was a mini CD player and a set of earphones. He gathered those up as well, and stuffed them into his shoulder pack. Couldn't have any anachronisms floating around to screw up the flow. Sure, anybody who found the paper might think it was a joke somebody had printed up, color or not, but the CD player? That would raise a few eyebrows. Maybe they'd think it was little green men from Mars—until they saw the "Made in Japan" label.

Atwood started his plea: "Look, Max, I'm not going to change a thing that matters, not a *thing*!" Sweat had beaded up on his balding brow. "The only ripples will be in my *own* swimming pool! I ran all the scenarios to the tenth decimal point."

Walker jerked his head upward for Atwood to stand. "Get up, Lyle."

He fumbled out of his chair to face Walker.

"Nice place," Walker said, and glanced around. "You couldn't have done this by yourself. Who supplied the ride?"

Atwood couldn't seem to stop smiling, as weak and unhappy as it looked. "I'm not *hurting* anyone, Max! It's America, you know? I just took a—an opportunity?"

Walker hated to see this, especially from Atwood. They had been friends, once. What seemed like a very long time ago.

He sighed again. "You're coming back," he said. There was no other way.

Bam! The door exploded inward, and two enormous men rushed in.

Bodyguards.

Atwood must have tripped some kind of an alarm—

Walker reached for his gun, then thought better of it. Neither man was armed. He moved his hand away from his pistol. You had to be careful with players you hadn't charted and didn't know. One of these goons could be the father or grandfather of somebody who mattered. Shoot him, and that could cause big troubles. Always a problem, trying to figure out if sneezing on the wrong person might butterfly its way through history and turn into a damned tornado down the line. Better to play it safe. He had his hands and his skills. Better to use them and keep from permanently damaging these two.

The first man into the room sported short, dark, slicked-down hair and a handlebar mustache. His lips were pressed in a tight line, and he raised his fists, palms inward in a quaint boxing style.

"I once went ten rounds with John L. Sullivan," he said, and started to circle his fists.

Walker wanted to shake his head. He was a boxing buff. Sullivan had been dead more than a decade, since the end of the Great War. This guy was maybe thirty-five. If he'd sparred with Sullivan, say, fifteen years ago, the old champion would have had to have been at least fifty-five and drunk most of the time by then.

Facing a real hero here.

Put up your dukes? Right.

Walker V-stepped to his left, rammed his right fist into Dukes's solar plexus, and hooked his right foot behind the man's heel in a fast sweep. The Marquis of Queensbury would have been horrified at the illegal and unsportsman-like move.

Dukes gasped, unable to breathe, and went down like a sack of bricks. He took one of the fluted lamps with him; glass shattered and the lamp snapped off at the base.

"You went ten with John L.? Hey, I saw Tyson beat Spinks on HBO," Walker said.

He spun, but not fast enough. The second man wore a snug vest over a long-sleeved white shirt; he wrapped his arms around Walker from behind and squeezed, lifted him off of the floor.

Walker struggled as Sleeves's vise grip tightened. Another second and his ribs would give.

Arches—

Walker threw himself to the left so that he faced one arched wall. He pushed out with his legs and his feet scraped at the arch, then found purchase. With Sleeves behind, he ran up the wall and broke the man's crushing grip. He finished the back somersault, landed behind

40

Sleeves, and double-kicked. Hit the confused Sleeves just behind the knees.

Sleeves went down. He cursed, rolled, and grabbed for the nearest weapon—the stem of the shattered lamp. He leapt up and swung the lamp clumsily at Walker. Walker dropped in a side split under the awkward swing. The metal rod missed cleanly.

Walker jerked himself up. He raised one leg high and came down on the hollow cast-metal stick with the heel of his boot, hard. The lamp pole snapped in two.

Before Sleeves could react, Walker reached out and took hold of the two ends of the lamp. He pulled them away, and used them like a set of *yawara* sticks.

He hit the man a dozen times, quick and snappy blows, to the ribs, the arms, his chest, working like a rock drummer on speed. As Sleeves crumpled to the floor, Walker delivered his final thrust to the groin. That would keep him down and clutching himself for a while. Probably still be able to father children, but not in the next few days . . .

And at the same second, he heard a sound that he had never thought he'd hear:

The click of a massive handgun chambering a round, a gun aimed at him by Lyle Atwood.

Shit! He lied!

Walker flung the sticks away and took a flying leap at the oak coffee table. He landed on one shoulder and rolled onto the floor. He pulled the table over on top of himself.

Gunfire exploded in the room. The table jerked and one of the legs splintered. Atwood was using something big and nasty, not likely a period .38 or low-velocity .45, probably a .40, if it was the same piece he had carried on the job for TEC—

Don't think, move!

Walker jumped from the crouch to take cover behind one of the heavy chairs—

The two shots blew the padded headrest into smoking pieces, missed his skull by centimeters.

Before Walker could pull his own gun, one of the doors swung open and a high, screechy voice called out, "Mr. Atwood, are you—?"

Walker saw Atwood spin to point at the intruding secretary. Walker ran past the door and slammed it closed, kept moving, a split second before Atwood sent three rounds through the thick wood.

Stupid—!

Running footsteps paired with sobs meant the secretary was still alive, at least.

While Atwood was distracted, Walker sprinted and dove, landed behind the desk. Several rounds pounded the desk— good thing they weren't armor-piercing—and Walker peeped around the edge as Atwood moved toward him, cautious.

Walker didn't want to kill him; he stood and faced Atwood.

"Hi, *partner*," Walker said.

"Ex-partner." Atwood centered the bore on Walker's chest. "Sorry." He pulled the trigger.

Click.

Lyle looked at the gun stupidly, then squeezed the trigger again. Nothing. He dropped the gun to the floor and looked up at Walker, gaze panicked.

"You never were real good with numbers," Walker said, and moved toward him. His ears still rang from the shots Lyle had fired—shots he'd counted very carefully.

Atwood's shoulders sagged as Walker faced him. They only had a minute or two before more people came in, but Walker wanted answers.

"Look, Max, if I leave the stock, just go, there's no damage! No damage, no crime." His sweaty face looked almost hopeful. "Nothing changes, nothing at all!"

This from the man who had just tried very hard to kill him, and yet he didn't feel the anger he knew he should have. Atwood was obviously desperate, and Walker knew what that felt like . . .

"I want a name, Lyle."

"It won't make any difference, in a few weeks this guy will run your whole world—"

Walker stepped closer, kissing distance. He towered over Atwood, who kept talking.

"If he doesn't get the money here, he'll get it somewhere else." His eyes brimmed with tears of self-pity and fear. "I can't tell you anything."

Walker raised one eyebrow. Atwood looked at him pathetically.

"He'll send someone back to wipe out my grandparents, Max! It'll be like I never existed! My mother, my father, wife, kids—my fuckin' *cat!*"

"Your cat . . ." Walker had never seen such an expression of despair. This from a man who once charged a doper hosing them with a submachine gun cooking on full auto. He'd been a brave man, then. Now he was begging. Walker wanted to throw up.

Lyle searched his face for some sign of concession, but Walker had no intention of letting it go, none at all.

"Shit!" Atwood looked down at his clenched fists, and something went out of him. "You ever hear the name Aaron McComb? Senator McComb?"

Walker scowled. "Bullshit."

"What the hell am I gonna lie for? He's running for President!" Atwood suddenly seemed desperate for Walker to believe him. "The man has tapped out his campaign fund, and if I don't make it, he'll send someone else! He already owns half the guys we work with!"

Walker frowned and leaned closer to Lyle. If it was true, this was big. "Point them out when we get back," he said.

"Are you fucking *kidding*? This guy will roll right over you, Max!" Lyle choked back tears. "If I go back and talk, it's my family."

Lyle looked straight into Walker's eyes, and Walker could see the man he had known as his partner beneath the fear. The man who only wanted to make his wife and kids happy . . .

"Listen to what I'm saying. My *family*. If I die here, it's only me. I'm not afraid to go, you know that. But my family . . ."

Walker felt for him. He sighed and rested his hands on Atwood's trembling shoulders. "You know I have to take you back," he said softly. "I've got no choice."

Lyle's face crumpled, and he dropped his gaze to the floor. "Neither do I," he said, so quietly that Walker almost didn't hear him.

Walker tensed, understanding, but too late.

Atwood ducked out from beneath his hands and sprinted for the window.

Walker moved. He was on him. He grabbed for Atwood's coat and ran with him.

They hit the window almost as one.

Walker grabbed Lyle's ankle as they plunged out into open air, ten stories up. He slammed his fist into his belt at the same time, hoped it wasn't too late—

The ground rushed at them, incredibly fast. Walker had time to register the upturned face of a cop as it all melted away, the cop's ruddy features spinning from shock to awe as the two plummeting men disappeared into thin air . . .

Five

Time Enforcement Commission:
Washington, D.C., 2004

Two uniformed guards walked on either side of Atwood, holding his cuffed arms.

Walker was with them. He tried to get Lyle's attention, but Atwood kept his blank stare on the tiled hallway floor. The hall smelled like a hospital. There was a hint of death in the air, though Walker knew that was only his imagination.

They were just outside the sentencing chamber when Walker nodded to the two guards, who moved a meter away from the shackled prisoner. The recycled air of the facility was cool, but Lyle still sweated heavily. He looked out of place in his twenties suit, his tie crooked, his collar open.

"Testify, and I'll do what I can," said Walker.

Atwood didn't look at him as he pushed the doors open with one shoulder and walked into the chamber. The guards moved forward to accompany him, and Walker followed.

There was no jury, no bailiff, no staff. The other TECs didn't even bother calling it a courtroom. Three judges sat behind a high black dais. The one in the middle, Korin Keech, had a gavel in her hand. She rapped it on the black counter and the quiet room got quieter; she was the supreme justice for TEC, and Walker knew what was coming if Atwood kept mum about McComb. Keech was fair, but TEC laws were severe—

Walker looked at Lyle, who still wore a dull look of resignation.

Keech spoke, her voice as cool as the air in the chamber. "Lyle Atwood, you're charged with violation of TEC code 40.8, subsection 9, time travel with intent to alter the present."

One of the uniformed officers stepped forward and placed Atwood's credentials in front of the judge. She looked them over, her expression firmly disapproving.

"The charges are compounded by your current status as a TE officer." Her gaze rested on Atwood.

"You know how serious this is," she continued, and her tone held an edge of something like sorrow. "Do you have a statement?"

Walker looked at Atwood. "Tell her," he whispered.

Lyle wouldn't look at him. "He only leaves you one way out," Atwood said softly. "I knew that. I took the risk. Sorry, Walker."

Dammit, just say the name! One word—

Keech raised her voice. "Mr. Atwood! Do you have something to say?"

Walker stared at Lyle. *Yes. Come on—*

"No, your honor." Walker's ex-partner slumped, but his jaw was set. "Nothing."

"Then I will pass sentence as mandated by our charter," said Keech, and she motioned for the other two judges to lean in. They spoke quietly.

Walker could feel his own desperation. "Lyle, *say* something!"

Keech looked up. "The defendant has been found guilty without extenuating circumstance . . ."

"They're gonna *kill* you, Lyle!"

Atwood watched the judge.

". . . therefore the mandatory sentence of death is to be carried out immediately."

Lyle glanced at Walker and smiled weakly. "Take care of yourself, Max."

Keech slammed her gavel down. It was over.

After it was over, after he'd seen the execution, Walker closed the door to the screening room behind him gently, unable to erase the image of Atwood from his mind. Unlike a civilian proceeding in a state or federal court, TEC rulings were final and swift. No appeal. After all, if something did turn up later to gainsay the crime, a TEC execution could be reversed. A man *could* be brought back from death—after a fashion.

Lyle had died quickly, within real-time hours of the sentence.

Walker started down the busy corridor, nodding absently to the officers who called his name in passing. He felt a tiredness that surpassed the physical aspect of exhaustion; his brain felt heavy, used up. With every death conviction, he hit the screening of the sentence; he didn't want ever to take his job lightly, and that meant seeing the consequences, no matter what. TEC kept them on file.

And they were filed forever in his memory.

Maybe he shouldn't have watched this one.

The monitor had shown Lyle appear in thin air, five stories up in front of the Floatbauer building, the time and date stamped on the corner of the screen. Within a few seconds of the time he and Walker had gone out through the window together. This time, Lyle was alone.

Falling . . .

He hit on his back, bounced, and died, internal organs ruptured by the sudden stop.

The cop Walker remembered from their jump stepped to the shattered body and put a newspaper over Lyle's face. No doubt thinking he was another rich broker wiped out by the stock market's crash.

So there it was. Atwood was dead. And through the intricacies of the *chronometric paradoxum,* executed more than forty years before he was actually born. The whole thing was enough to drive you crazy, but there it was. A jaunt back a year ago would find a younger version of Atwood, still working for TEC and bitching about it, but from this point on, he didn't exist. Crazy. Walker had learned to live with the impossibility of it.

He was stopped by the bulletin board outside of the squad room. A grinning, bearded face looked up at him. "Aaron McComb for President in 2004" was scrolled out at the bottom of the poster. Somebody kissing ass must have put the poster up.

Walker studied the picture, reached out to touch McComb's image. Cultured, sophisticated, and ruthless—if Atwood had told the truth.

Atwood died because of him. Walker was certain of it. The man hadn't had a reason to lie.

He stepped into the squad room, where Matuzak was briefing the group. He looked harried as usual, but in control. He was a good director and a good man. Hands-on, not just a political hack appointee who had never worked the streets. The boss was a cop's cop, come up through the ranks. Everybody respected him. When push came to shove, he was still a good man to have at your back. As good a friend as Walker had, though that wasn't saying much. He'd pulled into himself after . . . after . . .

Mat looked at Walker across the room, nodded, then went back to the smudged monitor at the front.

Walker moved past the scarred wooden tables and battered-looking computers to his own desk.

The room was too small to accommodate them comfortably, but their budget had gone steadily downward. Walker knew that the program was under consideration for renewal; they all bitched about it, but the tiny room and long hours for shit pay were the way it was right now. Word was, somebody was out to kill the unit.

And how many of these people are working for McComb?

Matuzak used a laser pen to point out a disturbance on the screen. "We're picking up some noise outside Camp David, '79; intelligence thinks it's a kill team out of Iran . . ."

One of the cops, a dark-haired young gun named Swerling, broke in. "If it is, that's their third try this year."

Problem with time travel was that other people had it. The only functioning chronometric gear on-line in the U.S. was under government supervision. The unit here and the original experimental station were the only officially listed units in the States. Probably the military branches had a station or two, under top secret wrap, of course. But other governments knew how the new toys worked, and they weren't so scrupulous about how they mucked around in the past.

Matuzak nodded. "CIA's tryin' to locate their launch and take it out." He stopped and peered at Walker closely.

"You look like shit," he said, not without sympathy. Matuzak had liked Atwood.

"We have to talk," said Walker.

"In a few minutes."

Walker gritted his teeth. He couldn't say anything in front of the others, not if McComb had some of them in his pocket. "Now."

Matuzak shrugged. "Okay, *two* minutes," he said, and turned back to the screen.

Walker dropped his paddle-holstered gun loudly on his desk

and then fell into his chair. A couple of minutes wouldn't make any difference, would it? They had plenty of time . . .

Matuzak went on. "I want two teams workin' the date, before and after." He started calling out names.

Walker looked at the one photo on his desk and felt another pain, an older one.

He reached out gently and stroked the image of Melissa's face, her features frozen into a smile ten years old, from the day she had died. She had said it, that he would be glad he had the picture. The words had haunted him through time . . .

Time travel with intent to alter the present, code 40.8/sub 9.

He searched again, as he had so many time before, for something in her smile that would tell him why it had to be this way.

I'm sorry, Melissa . . .

Matuzak had moved on to the second case. ". . . localized in L.A., 1902. Looks like we got someone trying to get a jump on the real estate gig. Purvis, you and Leroy."

The door opened. Everyone in the room looked up, including Walker. He heard Matuzak curse softly under his breath.

It was Spota, the President's lackey. He had with him a group of dignitaries and aides, undoubtedly to take what Matuzak called a "pocketbook tour."

And there was Senator McComb with them, arms crossed.

Walker had to fight to keep from reaching for his gun.

Matuzak finished up, his face neutral. "Uh, go over your dispatch notes, file your departures, and check with me before launch."

George Spota stepped in with a wide smile. His short dark hair was speckled with white. The job had aged him. "Good afternoon, gentlemen."

The officers stood up, and Spota led the tour over to

Matuzak. The men in suits took in the crowded squad room with thoughtful expressions.

Spota started with the introductions, but Walker had fixed his gaze on McComb's lean face.

"Senator Nelson, this is the TEC director, Eugene Matuzak. Senator Nelson is the newest member of the Oversight Committee, and we thought he might like to see how your annual budget is spent."

McComb moved closer to the group and then smiled coolly as he acknowledged Matuzak.

Walker could hear the ass-kissing in Spota's voice. "Senator McComb, our long-standing committee chairman, has graciously agreed to take time out of his busy campaign schedule to accompany us."

Bullshit politics. Matuzak knew who McComb was—the man who wanted to take the TEC down. What he didn't know was what else the man was into. Something that Walker was going to enjoy telling him.

"It'd be my pleasure to show you around," said Matuzak. Walker heard the well-hidden strain in his voice.

Nelson acted interested, very politically correct. "And are these your agents?" He asked the question as if speaking about a room of schoolchildren.

Matuzak nodded. "Most of them. Agent Shepard, Agent Timmons, Swerling . . ." Each of the officers bobbed their heads at Nelson.

". . . uh, Gordon, Agent Walker . . ."

McComb swiveled his head to meet Walker's stare. "Agent Walker . . . I've heard a lot about you."

The room went still and Walker shrugged faintly, let his stare get harder. "I've heard some things about you, too, Senator," he said, his voice without inflection.

McComb smiled. "Not all of it bad, I hope."

Walker let his silence and smile answer.

Matuzak broke in quickly.

"Uh, Agent Walker has just returned from a successful mission."

Senator Nelson smiled. "Well, congratulations, Agent Walker."

Walker didn't take his gaze off of McComb.

Matuzak kept talking. "If you'll follow me, gentlemen, I'll show you where we kick off."

The group was herded back toward the door, but McComb moved closer to Walker. The senator wore a polite, curious smile for the room, but his eyes told a different story.

"I'd love to hear a little more about your recent assignment, Agent Walker; why don't you join us?" His voice was innocent and pleasant, but his gaze was hard, sizing Walker up with a smooth intensity.

"I have a report to file—" Walker began.

Matuzak grinned at Walker, exposing too many teeth. "Agent Walker would be delighted, Senator."

Walker nodded slowly. Of course. Fucking *delighted.*

McComb gestured Walker to the door first with one slender hand as Matuzak hurried to the front of the group—McComb wore a smile that would freeze nitrogen.

"After you," he said, and Walker could hear the truth in his voice, sleek and polished as it was—McComb was dirty. The man reeked of guilt beneath his expensive cologne, and Walker was going to nail his ass to the fucking wall.

Might as well size him up now. Find out what the man was made of. Because after watching Lyle fall to his death more than eighty years in the past, he was damned sure going to take down the man responsible for it.

One way or another.

Six

Walker was good, but Aaron McComb had made his career on reading people, on being able to see past the facade.

He wasn't too happy with what he saw. Walker's hatred seeped past the cool gaze. Atwood had talked; he could see it in Walker's dead cold eyes.

Well. Too bad.

Too bad for Walker.

They started down the corridor behind the rest of the group. Walker hung back a bit, allowed the two of them to fall a few paces behind. Good; at least the man was discreet.

McComb's Secret Service agents backed off some to give them a little more privacy. Not too far. And they watched Walker, too. If he did anything sudden, the candidate's bodyguards would be on him like ugly on an ape.

Then again, this might still be salvageable. McComb owned enough cops to know most of them had their prices. A few carefully placed bucks might just grease this squeaky wheel away. Money always talked, and enough of it usually shouted down any opposition. It was better to *own* your enemy than fight him.

He'd find Walker's price and *poof!* End of problem.

Meanwhile that prick Matuzak was up there pitching Nelson. "As you can see, Senator, we have spared every expense. No comfort, no convenience, no necessities— watch your head there—"

They passed a gate that had "LOCK FOUR" printed across it in official-looking letters; at the base, a man with a screwdriver poked at a panel in the wall. Exposed girders and I-beams crossed overhead. It really was a stripped-down operation; nobody was getting fat around here. No, the extra money was being bled away much higher up the food chain; McComb had seen to that. He was even getting a little himself. Peanuts compared to what he was going to rake in once he got the job as head honcho. Money flowed to where the power was, and he was going to be the most powerful President ever. And then some.

Walker didn't say anything, so McComb decided to take the offensive.

"So, Agent Walker—your latest mission? Who were you after?"

Walker turned his cold eyes to McComb's—yeah, he was a tough one, or at least he thought of himself as such. They were going to dance a little. What the hell, it was something to do.

"A man named Atwood," said Walker. He had a European accent. French? Belgian, maybe? "Sound familiar?"

McComb walked on. "Atwood, Atwood . . ." He raised his voice slightly so that his aide, Lawrence, could hear. "Why should that name be familiar to me?"

Matuzak interrupted himself to call back. "Unfortunately, Atwood was a TEC agent."

"Really?" said Nelson, all ears.

54

Senator Nelson was a real loser, the fat fuck, but he played the game well enough to keep getting reelected. And McComb needed his vote. Better the moron you know than the moron you don't . . .

McComb kept his voice up. "That sort of thing happens. As a matter of fact, it's one of the dangers of even *having* an agency like this." Not really necessary, this whole little charade, but it would be interesting to see who took the bait.

George Spota cleared his throat, but kept his voice low and respectful. "Imagine the dangers of not having it," he offered.

Sharp as he was, Spota was on the way out, he was a lame duck, and everyone knew it, but still he tried. He was smart and that made him dangerous. McComb had no real use for him now, though the feeling wasn't malicious—it was just business. When he got the presidency, he was going to make certain that Spota went somewhere he couldn't do any damage. Alaska, maybe, or Peru, a nice job as a fry cook, or a deckhand on a fishing boat, maybe. Or a concrete overcoat and a nice room in Davy Jones's locker . . .

He grinned at the thought. Later. Right now he had more pressing matters to attend to.

"Did you know this Atwood?" His voice was mild. How much would it take to buy this guy? Couple hundred thousand? Chicken feed.

Walker loped along, obviously wanting to lean forward and scrape the ground with his knuckles. A mouth-breathing muscleman with a chip on his shoulder, how . . . funny.

"He was my partner," he said. His voice was clear and if not exactly cultured, at least educated. It clashed with the man's apparent stupidity. He had to know who McComb was, had to know the contrast was like a gnat against an elephant.

McComb shook his head in mock sadness. "Ah, too bad.

There's nothing worse than a rogue cop." Jesus, was this clown going to start spouting lines from an old Bogart movie about when a man's partner got killed? Guys like this went out with the dodo.

Walker looked at him squarely. "Except maybe the man who paid him to do it." He flashed a tight grin. Nasty.

McComb tilted his head skeptically. "If there *is* such a man."

The agent walked on. "There always is."

What was the expression, a fly in the ointment? This fly wanted to play a little before he got squashed. Fine. *Come into my parlor, little bug. Better say good-bye to your friends first.*

"Ah, I see. And do you know who this man is?"

"Oh, yes, I know." If looks could kill, McComb would have been a smoking lump on the floor. He guessed that if the cop had thought he could get away with it, he'd have pulled his gun and shot him by now. But the Secret Service guys would take him out if he went for a gun, cop or not. McComb didn't have much use for the Service muscle, he liked his own better, but the official heat had its uses. Everybody knew they were there and fast on the draw, all wired together with their little earplug radios into one big multiheaded unit, willing to die to save him from an assassin.

McComb smiled gently. "Then why don't you arrest him?"

Walker fired another glance of icy hatred at McComb and then looked away.

"I lost my witness," he said. Unreadable except for that look . . .

Now McComb loosed the sigh. "Too bad. I'm sure we'd all like to see the general in charge brought to justice instead of the common soldiers. I trust you'll keep working on it . . . ?"

Max Walker glared into him. "You can bet on it."

McComb kept his face neutral. No point in trying to bribe this one. He'd met a few along the way to whom money meant nothing, zealots who'd rather die poor for truth than live high and rich without it. This guy was one of those. A pity.

They walked on. Matuzak led them into a room full of monitors, the operations room. McComb hadn't really expected the agent to take an easy way out, and now there wouldn't be one. He was going to have to die. *So be it, chump.*

Too bad, so sad. McComb smiled.

Matuzak droned on. "We've updated our entire operation to state-of-the-art Parker Datalink Systems, utilizing their brand-new superconducting wetlight chip."

They all looked back at McComb with smiles of brown-nosing sympathy.

George Spota couldn't resist the opportunity to rub salt in the wound, even though they all knew the story. "As you know, Senator McComb sold his half of the Parker company just before they got the patent on the forerunner of that chip." He smiled sadly. "Bet that cost you a few billion, Senator."

McComb smiled a tight, embarrassed smile at Spota. He was fucking himself over, didn't he *know* that? Going to sleep with the fishes.

"Bad luck," said Walker smoothly.

"Win some, lose some." McComb said, as he stepped past him to address the group. Enough games.

"My concern is the taxpayers' money," he said. He was done playing nice. They wanted to poke at him, let them see what happened when he woke up. "At a time like this, when

57

so many of our citizens are unemployed or unprotected, I don't think we can afford to continue supporting a project like this—a project that might be more dangerous than the problems it claims to protect us from."

Senator Nelson frowned stupidly. "What dangers?"

McComb addressed the question as though it were an intelligent one. "Well, take dishonest agents like this . . . Atwood," he said. "They could take advantage of the situation for personal gain and in doing so wreck time. Even by accident, the ripple effect could cause problems in their future—our present. Look at a minor example for instance: When an agent goes back, he risks contact with a past version of himself—assuming he lands in his own life span—and from what I understand, that in itself could be a disaster."

Nelson wasn't going to get it without little words, big charts, and bright colors. Maybe not then. "Why?" he asked.

Matuzak stepped in, cutting off his query with a glare. "It's all in the technical reports." His voice was dismissive. "However, it's never happened. We're very careful."

McComb smiled winningly at Nelson, and saw that he was going to get the vote he wanted soon enough. "That's what they used to say at Three Mile Island. What I propose, Senator Nelson, is far less costly and accomplishes the same thing. *Prevent* time travel altogether rather than spend stupendous amounts policing it. You can't hurt what you can't get at. If nobody goes back, then nothing can be changed."

McComb nodded to Walker in mock politeness. "Now, gentlemen, I'm afraid I have to get back to the Hill. Senator," he smiled at Nelson again, "this is a project we can live without. I hope I'll have your vote against continued appropriations."

He looked at Walker again. "Agent Walker, I must admire

your dedication. I do hope you'll keep trying to get your man."

Walker didn't blink. He moved closer to McComb. "I never quit. You can bet your life on it, Senator."

McComb ignored him and followed Lawrence out of the room with a half bow to the group.

Oh, you're going to quit, all right.

McComb didn't laugh out loud until they were safely out of earshot.

The white limousine cut easily through the darkening D.C. streets. They passed the Capitol, its dome lights piercing the twilight as Lawrence prattled on from his side of the plush leather backseat. McComb idly fed himself salted peanuts from a cut glass bowl.

In the front, Palmer, McComb's security man, glared at the whiny aide, but Lawrence was, as usual, oblivious.

The Secret Service rode in the cars ahead and behind them. McComb only allowed his own people to ride with him. He could do this as a candidate. After he was elected, maybe not, but by then who cared? He could be as straight as a Texas interstate after he was in charge.

". . . figures in the suburbs are encouraging, but they're killing you in the urban centers . . ."

Walker reminded McComb of someone he had known a long, long time ago, from childhood. The neighborhood pet, a bright, athletic kid named Esterhaus, Tommy Esterhaus . . .

Tommy had run errands for old ladies, had a paper route, and been incredibly popular with the other parents—his name was mostly used in sentences that started with "Why can't you be more like Tommy . . ." The girls all thought he was dreamy.

Which had been no big deal; every neighborhood probably had a kid like that, the example held up to the rest of the kids. Until Tommy, who was a minister's son, decided to rat on a young Aaron McComb for some minor offense; McComb couldn't recall it exactly. Something about stealing something from another kid.

McComb had paid one of the larger school bullies twenty bucks to beat the shit out of Tommy. The young Mr. Sunshine had landed in the hospital with two broken ribs, a fractured jaw, and a face scarred for life. Not so dreamy after that, was he . . . ?

Kind of like Walker. Wonder where he got that scar.

The senator allowed a fleeting nostalgic pleasure at the thought of Tommy and ate another peanut. If only all his problems could be solved so simply . . .

Lawrence was still talking like a fucking idiot: ". . . a shift away from you in men under twenty-five and women over forty. And I'm not sure if we can come up with a plank that appeases both groups. On the other hand, you're gaining with the pro-ers, life and death penalty, and America for Americans." He frowned thoughtfully. "The bad news is, the campaign finance chairman put together a projected budget, and it's a big number, Senator. Even going back again, I don't know how you could get it all in time—"

McComb snapped. He didn't think, just grabbed Lawrence. A red, pounding haze filled the air, clouded his sight. He threw Lawrence's head as hard and as far as he could. The man's skull cracked, blood spattered the seat—

No. Not the skull. It was only the crack of glass against bone. And the cut was tiny, hardly anything.

Lawrence fell into the corner, cowered there, his scalp blood smeared on the tinted window.

McComb sighed.

Palmer smiled meanly, enjoying Lawrence's pain.

"Now—I love you, Lawrence, I really do," he said

patiently. "But *don't* tell me what I can't do. Never, *ever* tell me what I *can't* do. Elections are won with television. You don't need the *press,* you don't need *endorsements,* and you don't need the *truth;* Lawrence, all you need is money."

He studied his aide's bleeding face to see if he understood.

Lawrence nodded numbly, dazed perhaps.

"Now, what is it going to cost me to buy the network time I need?"

Lawrence spoke timidly. "Over fifty million dollars . . ." He shrank a bit farther into the corner, frightened.

"And Agent Walker has already cost me that much," McComb said. He looked at Palmer and smiled. "Before I send someone else back, I want us to have a little chat with Walker. The kind of talk a man remembers for a lifetime. However long or short that might be."

Palmer smiled back.

Lawrence touched his bleeding head in shock.

McComb went back to his peanuts. Hmm. A little too salty. He'd have to remind Lawrence to lighten up on that.

It had been a pretty good day, all in all.

Seven

Spota was a good guy, but he'd lost most of his clout—that had been clear in the past few months, but had gotten a fuck of a lot clearer after this afternoon's display. Spota had listened to McComb's little speech and hardly peeped. You didn't need to be a weatherman to know which way the wind was blowing.

Eugene Matuzak had worked his ass off to get where he was, and now it was all going to get flushed, if things didn't come off right. He'd spent the afternoon immersed in red-tape paperwork, forms signed and appeals sent out— and it still didn't look a whole lot better for the TEC.

Well, it ain't over yet.

Matuzak glanced at his watch, then shook it. It was over for tonight. Carol was gonna be pissed if he wasn't home in the next twenty minutes; she was doing something Asian with a chicken.

He stood and shouldered his suit coat. He looked at the mess of files on his desk and sighed. *Fucking computer age, my ass.*

It'll have to wait till tomorrow.

He walked out of his office and into the squad room, wincing at the full-on dark outside the windows. How had it gotten so late? Timmons was at her desk, glaring at her keyboard; Matuzak had assigned her another case, and she wasn't happy about it.

Max Walker was the only other cop in the room. He sat upright in his wooden chair, back to Matuzak, stare glued to his computer screen. The face and stats of Senator McComb were visible from where Matuzak stood.

Matuzak stepped closer. Walker's hands weren't anywhere near the controls; he studied McComb as if he were some kind of a test. As if he had to know every pore or he'd fail. Next to the computer was the cheap snapshot of Melissa Walker, taken on the day she had died. She had been a pretty girl . . .

Walker had joined the TEC after a short leave of absence following his wife's death; he had walked into the office the day after the hospital released him, ready to work. Walker had been Matuzak's first choice when he'd gotten the TEC assignment—they had worked together before, and Walker was good. No, he was better than that; Max Walker was clean and sharp, maybe the best Matuzak had ever seen. He was a man made for the uniform.

And you never got over her, Max . . . It had been what, ten *years*? Melissa's death had made him harder, colder— and a great cop. All Walker seemed to have in his life was the job. He was an administrator's dream, but on a personal level, Matuzak wished Walker could find someone or something to fill the void that she had left in him . . . They weren't friends, exactly, but they had worked together for a long time, and they were as close as Walker would allow.

McComb's cheesy-sincere grin seemed to hover above the screen. Matuzak moved closer.

64

"Sure is a handsome devil, isn't he?"

Walker didn't even look back. He would have known someone else was in the room immediately; he seemed to have a sixth sense about that kind of stuff.

"Not my type," said Walker, his lilting accent cool as iron in a snowstorm. "What do you know about him?"

Matuzak almost smiled. "Capable of eating his young."

No reaction from Walker. Matuzak frowned. "He sure seemed interested in you this afternoon . . ."

Walker didn't miss a beat. "Atwood named him."

Had he heard that correctly? He glanced over at Timmons, but she didn't look up. "You're shitting me."

Walker's voice was certain. "He's the one who sent him back."

Matuzak was surprised and confused. It wasn't like Walker to fuck around about—well, *anything,* but this was Aaron *McComb* for Christ's sake.

"So why didn't Atwood testify?"

Walker didn't move. "He said that McComb would go after his family." Walker looked back at Matuzak, finally, unreadable. "He said McComb has half the agency in his pocket. I believe him."

Matuzak studied Walker's lined and scarred face. No joke. "He doesn't have me," he said.

Walker didn't say a word.

Matuzak kept his voice down so Timmons wouldn't hear, but it wasn't easy. Did Walker really think that a prick like McComb could get to him?

"I *said,* he doesn't have me."

Walker turned back to the screen.

"Yeah, well, fuck you, too," said Matuzak, and readjusted his coat. There was enough shit on his plate already; he didn't need fucking Max Walker to add to it. He started to walk out.

Walker broke his silence. "He's gonna shut us down, Mat. Then no one can stop him from going back." He paused, and looked at the picture of Melissa. "Atwood didn't lie."

Walker believed that *he* was clean, at least. Matuzak turned and settled slowly into a chair next to Max's desk.

Walker seemed oblivious. "This one's mine," he said, straight into McComb's smiling image.

Matuzak felt a twinge of worry at the set of Walker's jaw. "Not unless I say it is," he said, his voice mild.

That got Walker's attention. He turned and glared.

"The son of a bitch is a presidential candidate, Walker. You haul him in front of that committee, and you'd better have enough evidence to plug up the fuckin' Potomac."

Something seemed to go out of the harshness in Walker's glare. "You believe me?"

Matuzak nodded thoughtfully. "I always believe you, Max. But you're not always right."

Walker didn't say anything, but his gaze flickered to the picture of Melissa again. He never talked about her, and Matuzak had only brought it up once in their ten years as TE officers, a few years back. Walker hadn't been ready, not then . . .

They had been staked out together on a tech job in '99, a computer lab that someone wanted raided. They had gotten back to 1968 an hour before the event and had waited together in a dark room, filled with tiny blinking lights and deathly silence. After the quiet had stretched far into double digits, Matuzak had casually brought up the subject of women.

"So, you seein' anybody new?"

No response. He looked over to see the dark shape that was Walker, leaned against a console, unholster his weapon and check it. Matuzak waited, searched the silence for the beginning of a conversation, but there was nothing. Walker reholstered his weapon and acted as though they were simply waiting. Matuzak started to say something else, but he saw the shadows of Walker's face—Max had closed his eyes, an expression of loss and anger on his tight features.

And that had been the end of it—until now. Matuzak took a deep breath. "Turn that machine off and come to the house for dinner. Carol would love to see you."

Walker seemed to consider it, and then shook his head. "Thanks, some other time."

Matuzak watched Max with the picture of his long-dead wife and tried again. "You're allowed to have a life, you know . . . I read it in a manual someplace."

Max reached out and touched the snapshot. Matuzak saw a look on his face that he couldn't recall Walker ever wearing before—tenderness, combined with a huge, wistful sadness. When he spoke, his voice was clear and soft.

"I loved her," he said simply. He opened his mouth to say more, then closed it again.

Matuzak didn't say anything.

Walker looked back at McComb, and the look was replaced by an intensity that was almost frightening. "I'll tell you this, Mat—if I can't go back to save her, this scumbag's not going back to steal *money*."

Matuzak nodded. If something happened to Carol or one of the kids, would he be able to keep himself from going back? Maybe. Walker was a strong man, stronger than he even knew—and he used that strength to keep himself sane.

Matuzak stood up and reached for his coat. "Go home," he said. "If you won't come to mine, go to yours."

Walker was already attached to the screen again.

Matuzak walked to the door and then looked back at the younger man, hunched over what his life was—a fading picture and the Job. Important work that needed doing, but it wasn't enough, not even for Walker—and there wasn't anything that Matuzak could do to help him jump the gap of all that emptiness.

"By the way," he said, and Walker looked over at him. "When I said, 'McComb hasn't bought me,' you were *supposed* to say, 'I know that.'"

Max smiled, a thin one. "I know that." He went back to the screen.

Matuzak smiled at him, nodded to Timmons, and walked out. When he got home, he was going to give Carol a kiss and thank God that he wasn't in Walker's shoes.

Eight

Walker slid behind the wheel of the squad car and reclined wearily against the headrest; it was late. He tossed the files he carried onto the passenger seat. Old cases, new ones, more things to fill his time.

"Home," he said, and closed his eyes as the computer flickered to life and took control of the vehicle. After a few seconds for vox and pix verification, the screen set into the dash centered a blinking light and the car pulled into traffic. Technology was wonderful, when it worked. Walker never quite trusted the computer, was sure it was going to plow him into a bus at speed someday, but fuck it, if it did, what did it really matter? He was living on borrowed time anyway. If he had any guts, he'd have eaten his gun a long time ago. Only one thing kept him from doing that. Melissa's killers were still out there. He couldn't check out until they were smoking ruins.

He glanced at the screen and then closed his eyes again. Yeah, home—an empty apartment, an empty bed . . .

The police scanner crackled to life. A low, pleasant female voice called out a B and E somewhere in the west hills, and one of the nightshifters pulled it. Walker was unreasonably irritated by the noise and snapped it off; he had done enough for the day.

Lyle, then McComb—That was enough, but there was always more. He patted his coat pocket to make sure that he had brought it with him; if he had forgotten, he would have gone back for it. For her. He had a copy of it, in a safe deposit box, in case anything ever happened to the picture.

Walker turned on the radio, desperate to stop the thoughts before they started in earnest.

". . . and that was the timeless sound of Body Count and their golden-oldie hit from '92, 'Cop Killer.' Brings back memories, don't it?"

Great. Walker reached over to turn the radio off as the DJ rambled on.

"And now a request for a song first recorded way back in the seventies, probably before most of you were born, asking that age old question—does anybody *really* know what time it is?"

Walker hesitated, then settled back into his seat as the old Chicago song started to play. It made him feel even more exhausted somehow, but he'd always liked the tune . . .

He watched the passing lights of D.C. as the auto-guide navigated him to the apartment. Melissa had always liked the old, quiet stuff—Beatles, Simon and Garfunkel, that *Tapestry* album. A smile touched the corner of his mouth. Once, on his birthday, she had sang an a cappella version of a Jimi Hendrix song over his cake; he liked Hendrix a lot, and the fact that she had been the tiniest bit tone-deaf had added to the charm. Christ, she must have listened to that song twenty times while he was at work, just to get the words down . . .

The squad car pulled into the heavily barred apartment complex he called home and slipped into the underground garage. He ignored the flaking paint and the rusted chains, as he always did. It was a place to sleep and keep his stuff, nothing more, and the one thing he could say for it was that the neighbors kept to themselves, which was how he wanted it.

The security gate squealed to a close behind him. Theoretically, it was safe to leave his car and walk though the garage. As if any bright nine-year-old kid with a buck's worth of electronics couldn't rascal the system and get inside.

Well. If somebody jumped out of the shadows, he was too tired to fight. He'd just shoot them and to hell with it.

Walker picked up his files and trudged up to his apartment. He fumbled for his key card and had to run it through the slot in his door three times before it beeped acceptance; he'd have to get a new card soon . . .

The safety light and answering machine clicked on as he stepped into the room. The machine's robotic voice droned at him as he walked through the empty apartment toward his desk. The door latched shut behind him.

"Hello. You have—no messages. None. Zip. Zero."

"Yeah, yeah, fuck you, too," he muttered, and dropped the files on the desk. He took off his jacket and gun and lay them across a chair. The photo fell out of his pocket and fluttered to land at his feet. Even Matuzak didn't know that he took it with him when he left the office . . .

He picked it up and looked around his home. A couch, workout equipment, a tiny kitchen nook with a water dispenser, and a TV screen set into a panel on the wall. Not much to look at, but it was all he needed to survive.

That's all he was doing. Surviving.

Sometimes he didn't feel as if he lived here, and in those moments, he could see what Melissa would have done. New paint, a coffee table with her magazines strewn across it, black-and-white photos of the world outside blown up and hung tastefully on the walls—and flowers, Melissa loved to press and dry flowers. She had favored those tiny purple ones, lavender or something. The air would have been soft and alive with their fragrance, and the apartment would have always been warm . . .

To do those things without her would make it worse, would turn it into hell.

And he had already been *there,* the night she had . . . had been . . .

"Television," he said abruptly, and the TV panel swirled with gray static. He needed to see her, couldn't stop himself, even though it reminded him again of all he had lost.

"Play CD."

The screen flickered, and there she was. He walked closer to her, not looking at the time stamp at the corner of the panel; he knew what it said and he didn't want it to be there—6/15/94, 6:20 P.M.

She wore his leather workman's apron and grinned up at the camera from her place on a pale bed sheet in their backyard. There was a large box across her lap with a picture of an assembled birdhouse on it, and the out-of-focus trees behind her sang with the late afternoon sounds of wind and bird song.

Her eyes twinkled at him, her soft hair pulled back, a smudge of dirt on one of her slender arms. She tilted the box upward slightly so the camera could read it: "Easy to Assemble Home Kit."

"It's going to look exactly like this when I'm finished," she said, and Walker reached out to touch the cool glass screen.

Another voice, a voice he hardly recognized as his own, spoke into the microphone. Melissa's image trembled a little.

"If it does, I'll move in." A much younger Max Walker, love and hope in that sound. Not him, not anymore.

Melissa dumped the contents of the box across the sheet and unfolded the "easy to assemble" instructions—a piece of paper roughly the size of a tablecloth. She started rummaging through the bits of wood with a gentle sigh.

Walker stepped back from the TV and stripped off his shirt. He threw it across the couch and then sat down next to it, his mind half-numbed. He scooped up a forty-pound dumbbell and started to curl it. He hadn't stretched, and the weight was a strain on cold muscles, but he didn't care.

Melissa ignored the directions for a moment and tried vainly to fit two of the wooden panels together. Walker started to feel the pull of the weight and switched arms. Curl. Curl. Veins stood out on his bicep.

The younger Walker spoke again, off screen. "You sure you don't want me to help?"

Melissa studied the instructions. "You can buy the birdseed," she said. "Let's see—separate the parts into groups determined by structural function . . ."

She looked up at the camera, out at a much older Max Walker, who pumped iron without really feeling anything but pain. Her face was set in lines of mock frustration and determination.

What do you see, 'Lis?

Her husband spoke with a grin from behind the camera. "I think I'll have to buy more videotape."

Melissa shrugged dismissively. "I didn't say I'd do it in record time." She looked back at the directions and read on.

"Birds are starting to circle," said the young Max. "Looks like vultures."

The old Max switched arms again. Sweat trickled down the back of his neck, but he didn't blink.

"Well, you have to be in the right mood for this," she said, and looked up again. This time a slight, seductive smile was spread across her face. She crooked one finger toward the camera, beckoning.

"You were in the right mood a second ago," said Max.

Her smile widened, and she dropped the instructions. "I think I should start with something easier to put together."

Curl. Curl. Breathe. Breathe.

The scene spun out of focus as the video camera was set down, still running. And Max Walker stepped onto the screen, the crazy angle somehow showing it all. No cruel scar twisted down his face, no tightness pulled at his features. He was young and in love and then embracing her, laughing. They fell backward together onto the sheet, and now he could only see their legs, intertwined.

Their voices were clear. "Shouldn't you lay out all the parts first?"

Melissa giggled. "I wanna try from memory. I just find part 'A' and work from there . . ."

Their legs twisted around and there were more giggles.

Walker hesitated on the next curl, strained to hear her final words.

"I love you, Max—" The barest whisper, followed by the sounds of their lovemaking.

Walker couldn't stop it, them, the rush of emotions at her words. The dumbbell slipped from his sweaty fingers and thumped to the floor.

He had seen the tape so many times that he had it memorized, and still, her sweet love for him ripped at his heart.

Without the job, he might have given up a long time before—the only things that kept him going were that the fuckers who had murdered that lovely woman had never been caught—and the knowledge that somewhere, sometime, she was still alive, still trying to get that birdhouse

74

together, still pressing her flowers. The job kept him sane because it reminded him every day that she was still out there.

God, if only he could go back! Go back and change things . . .

And the Devil sang to him as he had so many times before: *You can—*

No.

It went against everything he stood for, all that he had worked for. Melissa had died from a brutal incident that he couldn't change, not for himself—it would be wrong, and it might be a disaster. He couldn't be that selfish, to risk the future of the entire world for her, not even as much as he wanted to do it. There was no choice. He would give up the world for her, but she wouldn't live at such a cost.

He stood and walked to the bathroom to take a shower, wash the sweat off his body. The tape ran out and fuzzy static filled the dark apartment, guided him across the room. He called out and the screen switched to headline news.

". . . sources close to the McComb camp indicate that the senator is out of money and may be forced to withdraw from the presidential race. Here's John Ashley from the Capitol with more. John?"

Walker was too tired to care. The love of his life was dead, and all he could do was keep her ghost alive with video images and old pictures. She would always be young, beautiful, full of spirit—and a pale echo of reality.

Once again, as so many times before, he wanted to scream.

And in the background, the Devil sang his seductive song again, grinning into Walker's pain.

Nine

Walker died in a street for no reason and was led to a place of waiting. It was a huge room underground somewhere, the walls a pale gray, the shadows filled with gentle whispering shapes. The lighting was a soft glow, indirect; he couldn't spot the source. The temperature was neutral, not hot, not cold. He was alone.

Very alone.

He knew he was here for a reason. And, since it was obvious he was dead, the reason had to be one that concerned the afterlife, since there apparently was one. Why would he be here? It seemed obvious.

Walker turned to the dark archway of the room and waited for Melissa to come.

Other people walked through the archway, people he didn't know—but they somehow . . . vanished before they came fully into view. They came from nowhere—there was nothing beyond the door except darkness—and they disappeared into the air. The effect was that of a melting veil of faces and bodies, all of them smiling at his anticipation.

Where was she? How long did he have to wait for her?

He tried to call her name, but when he opened his mouth, only the barest whisper came out. When he walked toward the arch, he went nowhere; the arch remained the same distance away.

All right. He would wait. However long it took.

Finally, the people stopped stepping into the room. He strained to see into the air, but she wasn't there. He waited. He waited—

Hello. You have—no messages. None. Zip. Zero.

—What—?

Walker's eyes snapped open. There loomed a man, a weapon—

He grabbed for the Taser aimed at his face—

The bones of the assassin's wrist cracked as he bent them upward—

Two thin filament lines exploded from the barrel with an electric spark—

Walker rolled onto the floor. The barbed lines smacked into the couch centimeters from where his head had been a split second ago.

The shooter fell back, dropped the Taser, screamed—

Walker was on his feet. He saw two other men. With knives.

He sprinted to the semidark kitchen and ripped a drawer open. He heard the whine of the Taser recharging and snatched the first thing his hand touched.

He spun.

Knife One lunged forward, and Walker blocked—

With a *wooden spoon.*

Christ!

The blade hacked out splinters. Walker half-dropped, drove his elbow into K1's face, hard. The man flew backward, and Walker spun back to the drawer, jerked it out farther.

The carving knife. He wrapped his fingers tightly around it and turned back.

K1 tossed his knife from one hand to the other and grinned through long strands of greasy dark hair.

Walker was alert now. Three men, front door, him asleep on the couch—he faintly registered that the TV was still on and he was in his boxers.

K1 thrust, in-out, and Walker blocked. He shuffled backward and the blades cracked together. The man's hair was tossed wildly as he feinted in and got a shallow cut across Walker's chest.

He knew what he was doing. Walker felt the knife track open and drip.

The shooter still clutched his broken wrist, but the second knife man pulled a Taser of his own. Walker hopped back as K1 lunged again, and then he heard the snap of a Taser fired; the lines sizzled toward him in the dark—

Walker somersaulted out of range. He hit his bare feet on the floor and threw the knife by instinct.

—no time—

It thumped into the second man's chest with a hollow, wet sound, and Knife Two fell, Taser useless. He gurgled and slumped. Dead? It didn't matter, as long as he was out of it.

Walker's own blood dripped, ran down his body.

He didn't have a weapon now, though.

K1 moved in, drove Walker to leap for the couch. Walker found the towel from last night's shower and wrapped it around his fists, stretched it out between them—

He brought the towel up for the next vicious slash. He snapped the towel taut, blocked the wrist, threw a loop over the man's hand, jerked down, twisted the knife free.

He dropped the towel and slammed his forearms across the back of the man's neck. He used his crouched position to drive his knee repeatedly into K1's nose.

"Who are you?!" Walker shouted. He brought his knee up again. The man's broken face dripped blood across his thigh. "Who the fuck sent you?!"

From the corner of his sight, he saw the broken-wrist shooter step forward.

Shooter had his recharged Taser pointed at Walker.

Walker started to turn, realized there wasn't time. He stood, pulled K1 up in front of him—

And the Taser discharged, sent its lines into K1's throat. The man's body jiggled and spasmed as the high voltage coursed through him. Had time to think: Not fatal, if it was a legal unit, but he'd be out of it for a few minutes—

Walker was thrown backward by the shock. He crashed into the water dispenser and it went over, spewed a wave of cool liquid across the kitchen floor.

Walker brought his head up. Shooter jerked the barbed lines out of K1's neck; the man dropped. The Taser started its recharge.

Walker was dizzy, disoriented. He backed up, water puddled at his feet, and fell against the counter. He shook his head.

Shooter stepped closer. Grinned. His shoes smacked against the wet floor. He aimed the Taser with his good hand; his other hung limply at his side.

"Fifty-thousand volts, motherfucker!"

Walker dropped down into a crouch. Shooter lowered the barrel and squeezed—

—and Walker catapulted himself straight into the air, legs spread, and landed on the sharp-edged counter in a full side split.

The Taser darts hit the floor. The high voltage, transmitted by the water, crackled all around the shooter. He jerked as it ripped through his body, and was thrown back, shocked further by his vain attempt to get away—

Shooter flew back and hit the front door, cracked it, and crumpled into the hall.

Walker hovered on the counter, his own muscles locked, fists clenched. They were all down.

Good morning, Max.

"Shit."

There was movement in the hall. Walker twisted to look, but Shooter lay still. It was a tentative, hesitant stir; neighbor perhaps.

Walker vaulted off of the counter, careful of the water, although the Taser had already discharged. What the fuck had just happened?

And why?

He stepped to the splintered door and listened.

"Walker?" The voice was cool and female, and just on the other side.

Instinct had gotten him by so far this morning; it was the voice of a cop.

He moved into the hallway.

She was pretty in an intense way, her eyes wide but cautious. Mid to late twenties. She held a pistol and had flattened herself against the door frame.

Definitely cop.

"Walker?" she said again, this time addressed to him. He ignored her and watched the fallen Shooter, searched for signs of movement. The shock shouldn't have killed him—

He remembered that he was still in his underwear. The woman looked him over, taking no pains to hide her glance.

"Walker, I'm with Internal Affairs," she said, obviously the beginning of a speech. "My name is Sarah Fielding—"

Shooter groaned and started to move.

Fielding lowered her weapon, aimed it at the half-conscious man.

Walker looked at her and then back at Shooter. God, and he hadn't even had *coffee* yet. Hell of a way to wake up.

Walker glanced back into his apartment. How had they gotten in?

Maybe they had access to a sharp nine-year-old.

Outside, he heard sirens as the D.C. cops arrived. Somebody had called—probably to complain about the noise. The place was a wreck, a wet, smoking mess—not including the two injured and maybe even dying men splayed across his broken furniture.

He half-shrugged to Fielding. "He undecorated my apartment. Kill him."

Fielding darted a look at him to see if he was kidding. Let her figure it out; Walker turned and went back inside to find something to wear. Behind him, he could hear doors open and slam and the pitter-patter of little cop boots running up the stairs.

"Everybody freeze!" a man's voice shouted down the hallway.

Marvelous. A cop with a sense of humor.

Walker heard Fielding rustle through a pocket for her credentials. "They're all under arrest," she said firmly. "Assault, attempted murder—making a mess."

Walker glanced back into the hallway.

Fielding holstered her weapon and stood self-consciously, with her back to the open apartment. As he watched, she shot a curious glance over her shoulder and her gaze met his. She quickly looked away.

It was going to be an interesting day; even if he went back to bed and stayed there, he was already way ahead of the game.

Walker gazed at his watch and sighed.

It wasn't even seven in the morning yet.

Ten

Walker marched down the corridor to Matuzak's office. His head ached, and the thin cut across his chest was being rubbed raw by his uniform. The spray-on bandage stopped the bleeding but that was about it.

To top things off, Sarah I'm-with-IA Fielding was right on his ass.

He charged through the squad room, didn't acknowledge any of the TEC cops who milled around and ate takeout for lunch. He hit Matuzak's door, hard, and walked into the office. The door slammed closed behind him—directly in Fielding's eager face.

Matuzak looked up from his cluttered desk. "If you'd like, I'll have the door removed," he said mildly. Mat didn't rattle easily.

"I had company this morning," he said. He kept his voice as low as he could, but he was angry.

Matuzak studied his bruised face. "You look like they stayed awhile. What were they after?"

"McComb sent them."

He raised one eyebrow. "They say that?"

He scowled; it was so fucking obvious, he couldn't believe Mat had asked.

"*I* say that." He blew a blast of stale air. "And what does IA want with me?"

His boss had the decency to look uncomfortable, but he spoke as if he were explaining the deal to a rookie. "Atwood was your partner. Internal Affairs isn't convinced you can be . . . trusted anymore."

Fielding opened the door a crack behind him. Walker leaned back, and before she could step in, he slammed it in her face.

Speak of the devil. Walker gritted his teeth. "She is *not* following me around."

Matuzak looked through him. "We've got a phase four. You take it. It'll get you out of town."

Jesus, what did they need? "Get someone else. I want to be wherever McComb is."

"How about a little refresher course in agency etiquette, Walker? Whaddaya say?" He touched his own chest. "*I'm* the director. I authorize the missions." His voice went up in volume a notch. "*I* make the assignments, and this one is yours. Unless you'd rather dance with IA."

Fielding tried to push her way in again. Walker spun and slammed the door in her face a third time without thinking.

"Goddammit, Max! This agency isn't dead yet, but if I can't keep you out of McComb's face, it will be!" Matuzak glared at him, face red. "He wants us."

He looked at the door. "Fielding! Get in here!"

Walker lowered his voice, but not much. "She'll get in my way."

Matuzak half-smiled. "Well, then. Ask her to stand behind you." His tone dripped sarcasm.

Fielding eased the door open and stayed where she was.

Matuzak's voice went back to normal. "She's on the ride and you've got an hour till launch."

Fielding edged into the room and growled at Walker. "You're not funny, Walker."

He stared back at her. "No. I never am."

There was a loud buzz from the intercom. Mat jabbed at the receiver.

"Yeah?"

A crackling, urgent voice spilled into the room. "That disturbance just jumped from four, passed five, went to six."

Walker turned and half-ran into Fielding.

She scrambled to get out of his way.

Matuzak stood. Without another word, all three of them hurried out of the office.

Matuzak led them down the corridor toward the launch control room. Fielding stayed a few steps behind them, which was fine with Walker. He needed an IA investigation like he needed another asshole, and this woman was a fucking *bureaucrat,* not even a real cop; she had probably spent her street time writing tickets and busting jaywalkers, working her way up the ladder. It didn't matter that she was a woman—Walker had gotten over that in his twenties—it was that she was IA and didn't belong on an assignment in the field. End of story.

Matuzak took a right at the end of the hall. He barged into one of the small hacker offices, not bothering to knock. Due to funding, the various techs shared the few cubicles that had been set aside for their use. They were usually cluttered with clothes, food wrappers, and bits of paper strewn everywhere, and this one was no exception. It kind of reminded Walker of his own apartment as he'd left it earlier . . .

Ricky MacDonald, one of the better young techs, sat in

the desk chair, his back to the door. He wore a virtual reality headpiece, head down, and was heavily involved . . .

The three of them stood in the doorway and assessed the situation. Walker grinned, then laughed when he realized what Ricky was doing. Fielding looked at him, no comprehension on her pretty face.

"Oh—oh *yeah*," Ricky murmured, oblivious to their presence. His hips twitched and thumped in his chair, and he started to breathe faster. *"Yeah!"* He cupped his hands around thin air in front of him.

Matuzak moved across the room. He grabbed the helmet and lifted, breaking the connection.

Ricky, still aroused and only vaguely embarrassed, spun in his seat to face them. His face was flushed, but he grinned.

Walker laughed again; Ricky was famous for shit like this.

Ricky looked up. "Bad timing, Chief."

Matuzak scowled. "Ricky, I catch you fuckin' this machine on company time again, I'll break your neck."

Ricky looked to Walker for sympathy.

Walker shrugged. "It looked like safe sex to me," he said.

Matuzak dropped it with one final disgusted look at the tech. "Come on," he said, impatient. They were on a time line, after all . . .

The tech glanced almost wistfully at the discarded helmet and then led them out of the office and into the control center around the corner.

They walked past rows and rows of various technicians, busy confirming calculations and evaluating incoming data. The room was like the rest of the TEC facilities—battered and used. Streams of printout sheets and half-full cups of coffee competed for space on the consoles. Though it was illegal, there was a hint of tobacco smoke in the air, too.

Somebody was lighting up and trying to hide it. Walker didn't care if they burned their lungs out, but smoke could be dangerous around all this electronic stuff. Then again, as big a bunch of slobs as these guys were, it probably didn't matter. They probably spilled coffee and smeared donuts all over everything anyway. Some TEC agent was going to blow up in mid-leap someday because a wetlight board shorted out when somebody's breakfast crumbs gummed it up.

Given Walker's luck lately, it would probably be him.

He glanced up at the monitor board that dominated the control center. Although the pattern varied slightly each day, he'd always thought it looked like the rings in a tree, except green on black—each of the wavy rings symbolized a place in time. Walker had never quite grasped how the techs entered new info, or how most of the rest of it worked, but he knew more than the majority of the other TE cops. Given a few minutes, he could pinpoint disturbances almost as well as one of the hacks—

Ricky went to his own computer and sat down. There were tacky pictures and snapshots of nude women plastered all over his work space, alone and coupled. The plastic-pretty faces promised pure ecstasy, and their bodies were contorted into uncomfortable sexual positions. Ricky was a throwback to more oppressive times . . .

"Show me," said Matuzak.

Fielding and Walker peered over the tech's shoulder. He tapped the keys expertly and talked as he worked.

"So, the ripple was steady at four, then spiked up to six—I thought it was gonna stop at five, and that's bad enough—here." He pointed. "On the big board it looks like a killer wave set off Waimea, point of origin is here in D.C.—"

Walker looked up at the huge monitor. Yeah, it was big, he could see the disturbance waves at '94—

When Melissa died . . .

Matuzak sighed and spoke to Walker. "Shit. Go, you're outta here."

Walker nodded. In theory, if the probability spiked to an eight or nine, it wouldn't be something they could fix. It would be such a major screwup that their time would be damaged beyond repair. Something to do with the Grandfather Paradox, and Walker couldn't begin to understand the physics of it, but the bottom line was, if it got too big, it was like a tsunami, it would curl over the present like the Hawaiian surf Ricky was fond of talking about, only it would be ten stories high . . .

Walker and Matuzak turned to leave, but Fielding stayed where she was. The two men hesitated.

Fielding frowned at Ricky's photo collection.

"You should have an exhibit," she said. Her voice was colder than liquid nitrogen. The pictures offended her.

Ricky stared stupidly up at her, not getting it.

Walker smiled and wondered what the tech *was* thinking. Probably: *Gee, a real* live *woman! And she's pretty, too!*

"My really good stuff is at home," he said, voice dreamy and half-hopeful. It would have been funnier, except they were in a hurry.

Fielding shook her head and gave up, smiled tightly, and walked away, leaving Ricky to stare after her. He wore the same wistful expression he had worn looking at the reality helmet.

Walker shook his head. Some people never got it. In Ricky's case, probably that was literal.

Eleven

Walker stood by the armory rack in the ready room and watched while several technicians went through the calibration check on their equipment.

Great. "Our" equipment.

He didn't like that for shit. He didn't want another partner, especially this one.

Fielding waited for one of the techs to finish with her chestpack and then walked over to the gun rack. She thumbed the ID plate, then picked out an H&K .40, a little more pistol than Walker would have guessed, checked the magazine and action, then pulled a box of shells out of the lower cabinet. Her smooth features were a study in irritation, but she didn't look at him. She loaded two spare magazines, pressing the rounds into place with an offhand ease before she picked out a holster and the magazine carriers and clipped them to her belt.

"I really could care less whether you like me or not," she said in a low voice, "but you don't know anything about me."

Wonderful, they would have to seek counseling. "It's ten

minutes to launch," said Walker. Now was not the time to be saddled with an untried partner, no matter how much gun she thought she could carry.

Walker selected a weapon of his own. He picked one that matched his usual duty piece, a .45. It was not as hot as a .357, but the fat and slow-moving .45 would put a man down just fine. He popped the magazine, started loading it.

He knew that he was reacting harshly to the situation, even being rude, but he didn't particularly care. On top of the fact that her presence meant he was under official scrutiny, there was something about her—he couldn't tell how much of it was his own ego and how much was her, and he didn't have time to analyze it. But she was just . . . uncomfortable to be around. The feeling was the best he could do for an explanation. Something was wrong.

"I've been with IA two years," she said. "I'm field-rated class A in weapons and tactics, and I'm fluent in three languages." She paused and looked at him. "Now, aren't you impressed?" She ejected the HK's magazine, started to fill it.

"Blown away."

"I read the Atwood file," she continued. Her tone was getting nasty.

"You didn't mention that you could *read*," he said.

She ignored him. He caught a hint of perfume off of her, something flowery. "He was your friend and yet you still asked to go after him."

There was a question there. He kept his face blank. "It was my job. He crossed the line," he said.

"Or he crossed you," she answered.

Bitch.

They both slammed their loaded magazines into their weapons at the same instant. He glared at her, and she glared back. He holstered his weapon; she waited a second before she did the same with hers.

They were ready. He marched over to the side door and down the narrow white corridor that led to the launch bay.

She followed him.

He realized that he had harbored some vague hope that she'd get lost or maybe trip and break her leg or something. Obviously he hadn't gotten enough sleep. Ms. Class-A-speaks-three-languages was going to be on him like a wart, no help for it.

A few white-coated launch techs loitered in the hallway, and when Walker and Fielding passed them, one of them nodded to another. "She looks like the Vollmers," he stage-whispered.

Walker and Fielding both glanced back at them; the two techs were blatantly looking the IA agent up and down, gazes anxious.

Walker studied Fielding's features as they walked, then nodded. She *did* bear a resemblance . . .

Another tech, an older woman, stopped in her tracks and looked at Fielding, then dropped her gaze and hurried on.

Fielding turned to Walker. "Why is everyone so nervous? And what are the Vollmers?"

He kept moving. "When a launch goes wrong, the techs are the ones who scrape the wall. And you look like the Vollmer twins."

"Who are they?"

He smiled, but didn't answer. They stopped at the sealed blast doors, and a tech hurried over to punch in the security code. The entry slid open with a metallic grind.

They walked into the launch bay, a long, tunnel-like room crammed with electronic equipment. The din of machinery and people was deafening, effectively killing their conversation. The place reeked with the familiar scent of oil and sweat, and the white coats of the on-line techs were smeared with greasy handprints.

Heavy tracks, like a train's, ran down the center of the room. Fielding and Walker started toward the rails, which led to the readied launch pod. They walked past the red signs that lined the tunnel—"DANGER, EXTREMELY FLAMMABLE, NO OPEN FLAMES." Some joker had hand-drawn a smiley face on one, the inscription reading "Have A Happy Yesterday!"

A two-man car had been rolled into position at the top of the tracks; it looked like an escape pod on some alien spacecraft. Liquid oxygen hissed from the huge rocket motor, and it was chocked back on wooden blocks. On better days, Walker imagined that the car was a fighter plane, awaiting takeoff from an aircraft carrier; today he had a partner, like it or not. Of course, the exhaust was shunted and vented deep underground; otherwise, everybody in the room would look like burned soyburger after a launch.

Ricky MacDonald sat at the trajectory screen, his smudged glasses slightly askew. He was allergic to contact lenses, and too cheap to get the elective laser surgery. He turned to another technician, a mild-looking man seated at the launch control; Ricky had to shout to be heard over the noise.

"Are we gonna blast to the past?!" His voice was full of youthful enthusiasm.

Ricky was an idiot. Walker shook his head, wondering again how he could trust his ass to this clown.

The tech gave a thumbs-up. "Green for launch."

Walker and Fielding both climbed into the pod. Not a place to be if you had claustrophobia. Two techs came over to help them with the retractable restraints.

When he was safely strapped in—well, more or less—Walker looked over at Fielding. Her face was calm, but when she reached up to check the shoulder strap, her hand trembled. He raised one eyebrow but said nothing.

He reached over and flipped the com switch; the pod was filled with shouting tech voices.

"T-minus sixty seconds!"

"Fueling complete and clear lines!"

Walker looked ahead, to where the tracks dead-ended at a scorched and hammered-looking brick wall. From the corner of his vision, he saw the IA follow his gaze.

There were two identical smudges on the wall, dark and scrubbed-looking, with an undertone of brownish crimson.

Fielding shouted to be heard. "I ran dozens of launches, but I never noticed the colors on that wall before!"

How the fuck could she have missed it?

She caught his look and added, "*Simulated* launches!"

"Simulated?" He was surprised and even more irritated with the new information.

"Yeah! This is my first real one!"

Shit. No wonder she was shaky. "Don't stick your head out the window!" he shouted.

Blast-suited technicians started to pull switches. The enormous electrical pylons at the far end of the tracks sparked and glowed with arcing bolts of energy.

". . . T-minus thirty!"

"Circuitry complete and hot!"

Matuzak's voice crackled softly through the com. "She's a little jumpy," he said.

Walker glanced at Fielding. Her cheeks flushed, and she wouldn't meet his eyes. He looked over his shoulder to a control panel.

Matuzak and the young tech were reading the EKG, apparently unaware that they were being heard.

"Blood pressure is gonna loosen her teeth—and her pulse is pushing one-forty—"

Walker could hear the tight grin in Matuzak's voice. "If she farts, she'll get ahead of the pod."

Walker had to smile at that.

"T-minus twenty . . . nineteen . . . eighteen . . ."

Matuzak shouted into the com and Walker lowered the sound filter; Mat had underestimated the power of the mike.

"Fielding! It helps to concentrate on something serene during the launch!"

Walker looked over to see her reach one sweating palm into her chest pocket. She pulled out a photo, studied it, then wedged it into a crack on the control console.

It was a picture of a family—parents, kids, and a dog. She kept her gaze on it and spoke.

"Walker—what do you think about?"

He didn't blink. "Not swallowing my tongue."

The woman stared harder at the photo, with a laserlike intensity. Walker closed his eyes and started to deep-breathe, clearing his mind. He saw nothing, knew nothing except the Calm. Smooth sand. Breathe . . .

From far away, he heard Matuzak speak.

"How's Walker?"

"I'd have to shake him to be sure he's still awake." Incredulous.

Matuzak. "Oh, he's awake."

Countdown. Breathe.

Fielding shouted, "Have they ever lost a pod during a launch?" A voice full of panic.

Walker floated up from his meditative state to respond. "Ask the Vollmers."

"I'll do that! Where are they?!"

The techs were getting tensed. "Six . . . five . . ."

"We got polarity! We got a window!"

Walker grinned, and nodded at the battered wall at the far end of their ride. "See those two red spots?"

Comprehension dawned. He just had time to relish the way she squinched her eyes closed in mortal terror.

"Ignition!"

Flames boiled and the pod rocketed toward the wall. The G-force smacked them into their seats. In his mind's eye, Walker saw the flat plane of invisible energy fisted around them. The world curled inward and the red stains were about to destroy the pod—

Fielding screamed as the vortex spun and bent, the rising shriek high and piercing.

And then they were gone.

Twelve

There was nothing for a few years, or perhaps just a few seconds; it was dark and light at the same time, and Walker felt a sense of rushed movement in spite of the stillness. The silence was incredibly loud; even after all of the trips he'd made, the contradictions were unresolvable.

There was a sensation that he imagined as that of being squeezed by a veil of energy—the air rushed from his gut, and his head dropped forward in the nothingness. He could see himself from above, as if he watched a bad sci-fi movie about time travel in which he was the star.

And he fell into himself, complete and whole in a new time—

And he was dying, because there was no oxygen in this world, only a thick liquid atmosphere. Water—

His eyes snapped open. Fielding hovered next to him, her face panicked; no air, no life—

Fuck! He looked up at the surface of the water they had materialized in. He saw the realization in her eyes, and they both pushed upward.

They were barely a meter below the surface. They broke

through, gasped and spat. Walker tread water and looked around as his breathing calmed. They had landed in the Potomac, on the dock side of the warehouse district.

Actually, the *water* side of the dock.

"Goddamn Ricky," he said, for Fielding's benefit. Miscalculations happened, but MacDonald was too sharp to have landed them there by accident. With any luck, IA would investigate Ricky next, the little creep.

They swam for shore, the water cold. At least it wasn't as toxic as it was in 2004 . . .

They stumbled onto the riverbank. Walker pushed his wet hair back and started checking his equipment; nothing seemed to be missing or damaged.

Fielding was pissed. She stood and wrung water out of her sopping uniform. Water pattered to the sandy dirt. Her body was outlined by the material, and Walker couldn't help an admiring glance; she was in tight shape. Her abdomen and chest were well muscled, her limbs lean and firm . . .

He shook his head and reached for the locator. None of that.

"How're we supposed to dry off?" She was still wringing.

"Walk fast," he answered. He tapped the electronic device; no water in it, thank the gods. "Give me date and grid," he said into it.

She looked around curiously. Besides a few birds, they were alone. "Are we really where we're supposed to be?"

He watched the grid map and date appear on the lens. "Sunday, October 9, 1994," he mumbled. So far, so good. "Locate and route to disruption."

A tiny red line connected several points on the small lens. "We're close," he said.

He looked over at her. She had an odd expression that he couldn't place; nostalgia?

"The date mean something to you?"

She nodded. "I'll be sixteen tomorrow."

"Where?"

Fielding looked confused for a second. "Oh. I was living in Colorado." She frowned. "This is really weird."

She knew the rules, but he decided to remind her. "Don't get sentimental and try to visit yourself."

She half smiled. "I'd kinda like to call myself and tell me not to sleep with Bobby Trapasso after my party. I woke up the next morning wishing I was still a virgin."

He shrugged. "A smart woman would call Bobby and give *him* some advice."

He turned and started up the dirt trail that led to the street. She followed.

The industrial district was Sunday-quiet, the streets deserted except for the occasional empty truck. Walker checked the locator every few seconds to make certain they were headed in the right direction; the water had thrown his concentration off. Fielding hurried to catch up, but he kept his pace brisk. The sooner he could get this woman off his back, the better.

"So—how long was Atwood your partner?"

He didn't slow down. "Three years."

"Did you spend a lot of time together when you were off duty?"

He shot her a discouraging look. Did they have to do this *now*? "He spent his free time with his wife and kids."

She wasn't put off, but her tone became almost conversational. "Do you have a family?"

He felt his gut tighten and decided not to answer. He kept walking.

"Mine's still in Colorado. When my father started reading about time travel, he told me it was a bigger threat to the world than nuclear power . . ."

"He was right."

She went on. "Yeah, that's why I joined the commission. I mean, I think the whole world should be able to stay out late on Saturday night and not have to worry about whether or not the planet will still be there the next day."

He winced. Melissa had said something to that effect when he'd first told her about the TEC, that rainy afternoon so long ago—

He was surprised to hear himself respond. "You sound like a woman I knew," he said.

"Someone remarkable, I hope." Her voice was light.

He didn't look at her. "Nobody ever heard of her until she was killed."

When she spoke again, her tone was sincere. "I'm sorry," she said softly. "You must have thought about going back and changing that . . ."

He couldn't tell if she was trying to empathize or just doing her job, asking him if he would change reality for his own selfish use. He decided to end it before it got any further—why should he open up to this woman?

"Everyone lives with the past." He looked at her meaningfully. "You can't be a virgin again." He stopped and checked the grid. They were there.

He held up for a moment. They were at one side of the McComb & Parker Datalink factory. It was a large warehouse at the end of the block, next to an office supply building. Power ducts and steel pipes ran in and out of the structure, an elaborate refrigeration system. There was a funny smell in the air, like burned insulation.

Walker motioned for her to stay back, and he moved closer to the building, toward the front. A black stretch limo was parked in front, with senatorial plates—

McComb was part of this? Walker felt a rush of bitter satisfaction; maybe he wasn't off the case, after all.

He stepped back and walked to the rear of the warehouse,

Fielding behind. A narrow alley ran between the two buildings.

"McComb once owned a piece of this," he said.

She frowned. "What does that mean?"

"Money." He motioned to the dim alleyway. "Take the back and wait until I call it."

She looked nervous, but she tried to hide it with a brisk nod. "Got it."

He watched her turn and start to move off. What the hell, he didn't have to be a total bastard. She got a few steps away before he called out softly, "Hey."

She turned.

He smiled at her, hoped it looked semi-friendly. "Keep your head down. Tomorrow's your birthday."

She smiled, and started down the alley, drawing her piece.

He felt a little better about her—not much, but a little. He drew his own weapon and walked back to the front.

"Main Office" had been lettered across the door just past the limo. He crouched and duckwalked past the deserted car to the door, ears strained for any sound. The sun shone quietly down.

The office was empty. He tried the door—unlocked.

Maybe for once I got an easy assignment.

Yeah, right. He held his weapon ready and carefully slipped into the room.

He could hear voices raised from somewhere else, the factory perhaps. There was a set of metal stairs at the back of the cluttered office, leading up; whoever was talking was upstairs, the voice overshadowed by an echoing distance. At least two people, men. He headed for the steps.

He maneuvered past drafting tables, posted with complicated drawings. He looked at one; "Cryo-chip" was labeled

101

across the top of the schematic sketch. "Prototype" had been stamped on the drawing in red letters.

It had to be the superconducting computer chip that had broken up the company. In 1994. And if the time disturbance had anything to do with that . . .

Walker crept up the stairs. As he got closer to the second level, he could make out what the topic of discussion was.

". . . hey, it doesn't matter to me one way or the other!"

"And so you're going to take the whole goddamn company into bankruptcy?"

That voice. *Is that—?*

"We have a difference of opinion, that's all." Placating.

"Oh, I'd say so." Sarcastic. Powerful. A man not to be fucked with.

Aaron McComb.

Aha. McComb was involved in this time crime, and that told Walker a lot. If he was dirty here, he was dirty elsewhere.

He remembered all of a sudden the day when Richard Nixon died; that had been in this year, hadn't it? All the hand wringing and mealymouthed praise the man got after he croaked. The then-President, Clinton, decreed a day of mourning. People came out of the woodwork to talk about how Nixon hadn't been so bad, save for that one little mistake called Watergate.

Walker had shaken his head then, amazed. As if that one little mistake that soured the American public on its government were some kind of aberration. The logic that said the disgraced President had been squeaky clean until that one little slip was nothing short of astounding. You didn't turn into a major crook overnight. Nixon's deceit had been part of an ongoing pattern, the kind of thing men in control routinely did. Power corrupts. You begin to think you are better than everybody else, you are above the law, you can do no wrong—or if you do, you can cover it up, make it go away. What had happened to Nixon was, he'd finally gotten caught. It wasn't the first stop sign he'd ever run, and anybody who thought differently wasn't playing with a full deck.

Just like McComb. He was dirty, and this was just another dip in the mudhole.

Which was good. If Walker couldn't get him for one thing, he could get him for another.

As long as he got him.

Thirteen

The young Senator McComb glanced at his watch, feeling pure hate for the balding engineer who stood in front of him. They had built the company together, he and Jack Parker, and now Jack wanted to piss it all away on this piece of hardware—

Yeah, the cryo-chip was a good idea, no argument. But their money needed to go other places, to continue with their spec work on the Chen account. Parker was talking about a *big* fucking investment, not a couple of new computers; it would take years to work the bugs out of something like this . . .

Parker kept on. "It's the future of this company, Aaron. If you don't agree, you're welcome to just—walk away."

McComb looked around at the industrial work stations, the metal benches, the precision latches and electronic gear. To one side was the cold room, a glass enclosure, climate-controlled for experiments—this new chip, among other things.

Was this where his future lay? In this nitrogen-fed chop

shop, led by Jack Parker? Perhaps not . . . but he wasn't going to just *walk* away, either.

"Come up with the money to buy me out," he said. Parker was fucked for capital; they both knew it.

Parker scratched his thinning hair. "I can't really afford it—"

McComb started to smile. "Then what are we talking about, Jack? As long as I'm around, you aren't going to blow any more of *our* money."

Parker went on, produced a thick envelope from his pocket. "I can't afford it—but I found an enterprising banker with some faith in the future."

McComb studied Parker's set face, then reached for the offered packet, surprised.

"Take it, Aaron. You're out. You've got no faith in the company and I've got none in . . . *politicians.*" He said it as if it were a dirty word.

McComb rifled through the envelope thoughtfully. Yeah, okay—let the little man have his pipe dream. It was enough money for him to—

He frowned and looked up at the same time Parker did. There was a weird, electric humming noise that had suddenly built out of nothing.

The factory was closed. A power surge of some kind—?

The air seemed to condense, to *thicken* in front of them. McComb spun. Behind them, too—an arc of electric light shot through the apparition of density, followed by more. Crackles and hisses, and a heavy waft of ozone scented the room.

Oh, shit—

"What—?" started Parker.

McComb felt the icy grip of terror at his throat. The air congealed, took form—

—and suddenly two burly men just *appeared,* like

somebody beaming down from an old sci-fi episode. The two men were heavily armed. They looked like security agents, thin-lipped and glaring, the weapons trained on McComb and Parker—

McComb was amazed, terrified; he couldn't think. More shimmer, another materialization. Two additional men stood there, one a heavyset guard, his hand bandaged, a mean smile on his rugged face. God, what was this? Some kind of hallucination? Were they gonna *die*—

The second man grinned and stepped forward a little; he spoke to Parker calmly, as if he hadn't just *blinked* into existence from *nowhere*—

"Hey, Jack. It's been a while."

McComb could *feel* his eyes widen. That face—

Parker stumbled backward, bumped solidly into one of the armed men behind them. His shocked expression proved that this was real, at least he could see it, too.

But it can't be real! It can't!

The grinning man was—

—was bearded and well postured, wore a nice suit. Expensive Italian leather shoes. Gold and diamond cuff links. A banker, CEO, or a politician, somebody with class and money.

And beneath graying hair and a lined brow, he also wore McComb's own face.

Senator McComb grinned even wider at the stunned look on Parker's stupid mug. "Jack, it's *me*." He pointed at his younger self. "I mean it's him. Us."

He started to laugh. He didn't look at the younger version of himself quite yet; this was too much fun.

God, Parker looked so *young!* He'd forgotten that Jack had started to go bald at such an early age.

"Where'd you come from? What is this? You supposed to be his father or something?"

Jesus, Jack was in a stone-cold panic; his *father?* "Do I look that old?" He smiled to show he wasn't really hurt by the slight, then laughed again.

McComb turned finally to address the younger version of himself. He thought he had aged pretty well, overall, although the young man in front of him was definitely a picture of athletic health—

The young senator raised trembling hands, and when he spoke, his voice carried a whine of terror. "I don't know Jack's business. I'm— Hurting me is a federal offense! I'm—I'm a United States senator . . ."

He trailed off, and studied McComb's face fearfully. Dread didn't sit well on his young features.

McComb was embarrassed by the naked fear. "Jesus, get a grip. I remember myself with bigger balls."

He studied his younger self, and touched his own face, pulled at the excess skin on his jawline. "I gotta get this fixed," he said to himself—

Now that's *funny—talking to myself again.* He grinned.

His young self stepped closer. "Are we cousins?" It was a stupid question, but his tone was doubtful and the fear had dwindled somewhat. He reached out toward his older self—

McComb pulled back. "Don't touch," he said. "Same matter can't occupy the same space. Could be a big problem, very nasty."

He saw the first flicker of comprehension in the young man's eyes.

Good.

The young senator frowned. "Same matter . . ."

McComb helped him along. "You've got a special NSA briefing coming up. Secret session."

"But that's not for another week—"

The older McComb nodded. "Someone will say 'time travel' and it'll get a big laugh. Listen carefully. Take notes. Don't be one of those braying like jackasses. Trust me on this."

He got it. McComb could almost see a light bulb appear over the younger man's head.

"Christ," he half whispered. "You're . . . you're *me*."

After the initial shock, Parker had watched the whole thing with an engineer's curiosity. He stepped forward, a faint, quizzical furrow on his brow; both McCombs had come to hate that look. Well, there was really only one of him, but for the moment, it was easier to think of the young man there as a separate person. He was looking at him, after all, not a mirror.

Parker spoke. "How far back have you come?"

The elder senator couldn't contain his contempt for the man anymore, this sniveling whiz kid. Jack Parker had robbed him of potential *billions*—

He wheeled around and jerked his pistol out from under his jacket. The gun came up, flat, and smashed into the side of Parker's stupid skull. He could feel the man's flesh separate and shred beneath the grips.

Parker crumpled back and down, face bloody and dazed. Went to one knee.

God, this was good, so good. "Never interrupt me when I'm talking to myself," he said. To Parker's credit, he hadn't started to cry or anything—

He stood over his fallen ex-partner, weapon raised. "You're a visionary, Jack. Computer market was saturated, software stocks were in the toilet, and you knew you had something, didn't you? Your fucking 'coldware' revolutionizes the fucking industry, and you knew and didn't let *me* know. You didn't want to be associated with *politicians*."

McComb paused and glanced back at his younger image.

The youthful McComb watched, eagerly snatched each word and filed it.

Had he thought he was unreadable at that age? Christ, he was an open book. One with large print and small words. See Aaron think. Think, Aaron, think!

Ah, well. He would get better.

He looked back at Jack Parker.

"I came back to tell you that I made a big mistake. And I changed my mind. Oh, and if it's any consolation, the next generation of chips—wetlight, they'll call them—is responsible for us being here. So blame yourself."

He smiled apologetically and thought about what else he wanted Jack to know before he blew his brains out. Perhaps that his children would now never be born—he could tell him what wonderful people they would have been . . .

He pondered these things and then shrugged. It didn't really matter. McComb had opened his mouth to say good-bye—

—when someone shouted from the catwalk.

"Freeze!"

The older senator alone recognized the accented voice; he glanced up anyway.

Yep. Who should be there but TEC Agent Max Walker, with a gun pointed right at McComb's chest. The older McComb, too.

Well, shit. This didn't help things. Not at all. The man had a way of getting underfoot. Kind of like a roach.

It was definitely time to step on the bastard. Only, he had the drop on them.

Well. Time would tell, wouldn't it?

Fourteen

Walker crept along the narrow catwalk and watched, shielded from below by a cluster of conduits. When the elder McComb put in his appearance, he had to resist the urge to intervene with a quick spray of bullets. TEC would nail his ass for sure, he did that. But he had the sucker. The law was the law, and now for sure he would see McComb in the sentencing chamber. He edged closer, to witness as much of it as he could . . .

He wasn't particularly surprised to see McComb, not after he understood what the issue was between the young McComb and Parker. Walker moved closer still, cool and steady. Always, it was "Follow the money."

The second that the old McComb pistol-whipped the young engineer, Walker tensed. He raised his weapon and tapped his suit com link. He reached out for support and barely avoided a nasty burn; several of the pipes that ran up through the walk were iced with condensation. "Do Not Touch" was stenciled next to each of the frozen tubes, as was "Liquid Nitrogen."

Walker leaned into the shadows and whispered into the voice link. "Fielding?"

The older senator was rambling on about how he had made a mistake. The dazed Parker was huddled on the floor, blood running down his head.

Walker heard faint scratching sounds over the com, and Fielding's whispered response was frantic. "The lock is *stuck,* I can't—"

"We're gonna have to take 'em," he said.

"How long have I got?"

Walker stepped into the open area of the catwalk and leveled his weapon. The old McComb was right in his sights. "Now," he said into the link; she'd have to catch up later.

He raised his voice. *"Freeze!"*

They all looked up. The younger McComb looked as if he'd been caught with his hand in the cookie jar; his older self looked as if he could piss ice cubes, not an inflection of alarm on his features.

"Agent Walker," the McComb he knew said, his tone polished and smooth. "Do you know how inappropriate that word is?" He kept his pistol aimed at the fallen man. "Do we look frozen to you?"

Fine, he wanted to play. Walker didn't miss a beat. "You look like shit to me. Move and you'll be *dead* shit."

He turned his attention to the younger McComb: "Get away from him, *now.* The rest of you, drop your weapons. *Move!*"

The junior senator backed off as Parker struggled to get to his feet. The two bodyguards and the other man looked to their leader. McComb nodded and placed his pistol on the floor; the others followed suit.

"Mr. Parker," called Walker, "under McComb's jacket,

there's a track and recover module." He gestured at the older senator. "Throw it up here."

McComb gritted his teeth, the first inkling of anxiety on a face accustomed to getting its way.

Get used to it, Senator. It's all downhill from here.

Parker retrieved the module.

The older McComb smiled winningly up at Walker. "You gonna leave me back here?"

Walker returned the grin, gun never moving. "You're an important man, McComb. I need a river of evidence to make this case. You just handed me a nice, big bucket."

The disoriented Parker tossed the electronic pad up to him. Walker snagged it with one hand and then laid it gently on the catwalk.

"I wouldn't want you to disappear on me while I'm fillin' it," he continued. He looked over at McComb's personal bodyguard, Palmer. The man's arm was bandaged, a broken wrist—

Shooter. He had tried to kill Walker only a few hours before; it seemed like years. "Out for good behavior, Palmer?" No surprise he was here, a senator's bodyguard would have been sprung before the laser printer spat out the arrest sheet. So much for blind justice.

The older McComb shook his head slightly at Palmer, then spoke to Walker. "I'm not going anywhere," he said. "I want to see how you're going to get from up there to down here and keep that gun on us; are you going to float down like a feather?"

"Maybe I'll just shoot you first."

"I don't think you will. You're too much the good cop. You'd like to see me dead, but you want to do it legally, don't you?"

Walker saw Fielding enter the back of the room, her

weapon pointed at McComb and his crew. He grinned. "You like surprises, Senator?"

"Can't say I do."

"Too bad," Fielding said clearly.

The men turned suddenly at her words.

Perfect. Walker slipped under the catwalk railing, tucked his gun away, suspended himself by his hands, then dropped lightly to the floor. He pulled the .45, retrained his gun on the younger McComb, and moved toward him.

"May I have the envelope, please?" he said.

The junior senator handed it over hesitantly.

Fielding circled the group to stand next to Walker, her expression grim.

The older McComb started his pitch.

Walker had expected one, would have been disappointed not to hear it.

"Look, Walker—" he started, gaze intent. "The country is going down the toilet because of the special interests. We need someone in the White House with so much influence—"

—meaning money—

"—that he doesn't need to listen to anyone. That man could concentrate his full attention on the United States—"

Fielding motioned at the envelope in Walker's hand. "What's that?"

"The senator was having a fund-raiser."

He'd heard enough, but the older McComb wasn't finished. "Come on. In politics, an honest man's a freak—an ineffective freak, too. You have to go along to get along. To do the job, you need the votes, to get the votes, you need money and power. You've been around long enough to know that, haven't you?"

He smiled his vote-for-me smirk again, seemingly happy with the situation. "When I'm in office, it's gonna be like the eighties—the rich'll get richer, the rest will immigrate to Mexico to have a better life. This country is based on a pure economic principle, and I'd never try to change that. You going or staying? Listen, the future is coming, Walker, and you have to plan ahead."

McComb had dropped his hands as he spoke, his demeanor one of friendly collusion.

He ought to have been more worried than he was, given the situation. Why wasn't he?

Walker raised his sights to nestle between the man's dark eyes.

"I think you plan too far ahead," he said. He wasn't going to kill him; just take him back, drag his lies out for the TEC to hold up to the light. A quick death here was too good for him. Destroying him politically first was worse. Making him suffer in the spotlight, that was much, *much* worse for a man like McComb. *Then* he could go the way of all flesh—

Click.

Walker smelled the gunmetal a millisecond before he felt the muzzle of Sarah Fielding's weapon pressed against his temple. Heard the squeeze-cocker's arming spring as if it were a vault door slamming shut.

Uh-oh.

"Obviously *you* don't plan far enough ahead," she said.

Shit! He had sensed something wrong about her.

She was one of McComb's. She'd sold out—

She reached over and plucked his weapon out of his hand.

"Anything else you want to tell me about yourself?" said Walker. "You cheat at cards? Fake orgasm? Kick your dog?"

Palmer stepped up behind him and grabbed his arms roughly, pinned his elbows close together. His body still ached from earlier—this didn't make him feel any better.

Parker stood perfectly still, watched with haunted eyes. Blood had dried his eyes into a sticky mask. The older

McComb nodded toward him and spoke dismissively, as if he were an attendee at a dull party: "Let's finish up and get out of here, shall we?"

Fielding shrugged at Walker. "He's running for President," she said simply. "I'm voting early."

Palmer's foul breath sprayed Walker's face; the broken wrist didn't seemed to have hurt his grip—fairly amazing. He squeezed harder.

"Hey, don't tell anyone I killed you, okay? I'm out on bail, you know. It would look bad."

The older senator took Fielding's gun and checked it. She kept Walker's piece.

Walker turned his head toward the crooked IA agent. "Atwood took a death sentence because he knew McComb would kill him anyway," he said. Maybe he could still get through to her, at least to—

He cut off as the older senator raised the weapon and held it centimeters from Jack Parker's nose. The engineer didn't have time to say a word—

"Good seein' you again, Jack," said McComb. He pulled the trigger.

The weapon boomed, and Jack Parker's face blew out the back of his skull. Chunks of bone and tissue smacked across the console behind him. The glistening wet, still-quivering brain matter spattered softly to the floor, and he convulsed in his own gore to lie at his executioner's feet.

Shit.

The younger McComb flashed a greasy smile, his brow beaded with sweat. He swallowed several times.

Fielding's face went a ghostly pale.

Walker looked at her. "Maybe he'll calm down after the election," he said.

The brutal murder had an amazing effect on the older senator. He grinned at Walker and bounced the smoking gun in his hand. Walker saw a tiny spray of red across the senator's cheek.

"What's the big deal? Point it, pull the trigger"— McComb giggled and pointed the gun at Parker's corpse— "and boom, somebody dies."

He turned back to Walker with the weapon and stepped toward him. McComb pointed it at his chest and moved closer, and in that second, Walker realized that McComb wasn't just fighting for power—deep in the man's eyes, he saw a pure, malicious insanity. Christ, he was as crazy as the main room in Bellevue. Somewhere along the way, he had gone over the edge. He was *enjoying* this—the battery, the killing—as much as he seemed to enjoy politics. The man was a ghoul.

Walker prepared himself to die. And if he was going down, he was going to go down swinging.

Fifteen

Walker arched his back against Palmer and dug his elbows into the man's sternum. At the same time, he lashed out with a front kick.

The kick caught the old McComb's arm. The gun went off, and the misdirected shot shattered a wall of glass directly behind them.

A geyser of liquid nitrogen erupted from a broken pipe and sprayed out across the room. Walker felt the blast of frigid air as everyone dove out of the way. Icy white clouds billowed, fogging his vision.

He spun loose from Palmer and turned, struck hard—two, three blows to the face. The freezing fog was everywhere; it fuzzed Walker's sight, but he saw Palmer spit blood and go down.

Another shape rushed at him, grabbed clumsily at his arms. He dropped back and scythed a hard spinning kick.

It connected solidly with the junior senator's face. Very satisfying.

The young McComb reeled back, a fresh, bleeding gash across his cheek.

Walker crouched and shot a glance into the hissing, vaporous haze just as the older McComb stepped forward. Even in the confusion, Walker could see a twisted scar, faded-white on his face, on his cheek, where Walker had left it. Amazing.

The healed McComb pointed a gun at Walker and then hesitated. He raised a tentative hand to finger his new scar, one he'd had for ten years but not for ten seconds. He looked at his younger self, confused. It only lasted a second, and then he turned back to shoot—

Walker dove under the spewing icy plumes and rolled out of the line of fire— Two rounds smacked the cement behind him. He heard the elder McComb shout orders, his formerly controlled voice now crazed.

"*Get* him, goddammit! Kill him!"

The two guards were on the other side of the nitrogen stream. Walker saw that one of them had lost his gun, knocked loose by the ice; his cuff was solid white. The liquid pooling on the floor looked like steaming water, clear, clean—

They started for him. He ducked through the tables of equipment, head down.

He heard the older McComb scream for Palmer to get up and get the tracking module on the fucking catwalk—!

He risked a glance back. Fielding had stayed with the senior McComb.

The guards had split up. One of them was about to walk right up his ass—

The armed guard skirted a metal lathe—

Walker dropped onto his own back and swung his legs out. He caught the man's legs with his own in a scissor hold, twisted—

Guard One went down, gun lost, and Walker bounced to his feet.

Unfortunately, One bounced right up with him, unshaken by the fall. He got in a series of sharp kicks and inside elbow jabs before the guard spotted a new weapon.

He grabbed an iron pry-bar off of the lathe and flailed at Walker with it—

Walker dropped, ducked under the bar. The heavy metal crashed into circuitry and caught. He took advantage of his lowered position to hit One with a quick set of strikes to the stomach and chin. He felt the big man lose his wind as he smacked a final punch into his unprotected solar plexus.

Guard One stumbled back. Walker swept him to the floor and smacked the man's head into the cement, hard enough to put him out for a while.

Crack!

A bullet hit the floor next to Walker, then another. He dodged—

The shots came from above—

Palmer, catwalk—

As Walker doglegged, Guard Two took a running jump at him. He was bigger than One—he hit, clutched; they crashed to the floor together. They rolled and kicked at each other. Walker tried to get a good grip, but the man had had some training; he pulled out of Walker's grasp. They half rose, their struggle driving them toward the stream of freezing nitrogen.

Two was competent. The man with the iced cuff delivered a hail of blows and kicks, which Walker partially blocked and returned, harder. They danced back and forth, the temperature well below zero at their feet.

Two was getting tired. He pulled back, gasped—

—and spotted his weapon within reach on the icy floor. Streams of white smoke churned around it, and his eyes lit up. The shimmering metal gun lay there.

Two didn't think; Walker didn't stop him. Two grinned

121

with anticipation, dropped to his knees, and scooped up the fallen pistol—

His face collapsed into confusion and then agony as his hand froze to the metal, burning him as much as if it had been red-hot. He howled in pain.

Even in his anguish, Two pulled himself to his feet. He raised the frozen weapon and tried to aim it—

Walker was already in motion. He had stepped back and now leapt at the guard feet-first, aimed at the man's chest. The flying kick drove Two backward, all control gone. The guard flailed into a steel pipe—

—and started to scream in earnest. The side of his face had slapped against the pipe and stuck there. He gained twenty, forty, sixty years as his hair frosted white under the leaking nitrogen and his skin began to blister around the contact point. The moisture from his shrieks froze and choked him as he grew a beard of white and his breathing passages stopped up.

He ceased to scream as his head started to freeze solid. *Jesus.*

Walker fell back when another round from the catwalk cracked into the brittle cement—

Palmer stopped to reload.

Walker ducked back under the walk.

Fielding was nowhere, but both of the McCombs stood at the foot of the metal stairs. From where he crouched, Walker could make out most of what they said.

The older McComb handed over a manila packet and talked fast. "You own the company, chip's gonna be worth billions. Read this and do what it says, you won't regret it. Now get the hell out of here, go, *leave!*"

As the young senator started for the door to the main office, his older self called out, "Hey, do me a favor—lay off the candy bars!" He patted his small belly, then started up the stairs.

Fucking piece of shit— He could joke right now, after slaying an old friend and watching his own men die.

Palmer had reloaded and fired vague shots in Walker's direction.

Walker spun, dodged, looked wildly for *something*—

There! A thick, rubber-coated wire ran to a piece of nearby equipment, "440 Volts" written plainly on the panel. A big power line. Walker ripped the three-cord wire loose and yanked. The cord came out, raw ends split—

The young McComb was gone, damage done; the other, older version of him was almost to the top of the metal stairs.

Palmer fired again, closer, and narrowly missed Walker's head—he heard the bullet buzz past like a crazed hornet—

Jesus I hope this works—

Walker grounded the bare ends of the wire against the metal struts that ran to the catwalk. There came a flash of sparks and a burnt ozone stench—

Palmer howled like a stuck dog, gun down, his hands plastered to the frying metal rail. He shook and rattled.

The jolt of current also knocked the senator halfway back down the steps, and he moaned.

They were down. Walker dropped the shorted-out cord to the cement, where it writhed like a broken-backed snake. He climbed up and through the equipment tables to reach the catwalk, then vaulted onto the suspended platform.

Palmer had recovered, at least partially. As Walker got his balance, the security man bent and snatched his gun off the walk. He brought it up—

Walker was close. He whipped out with a kick, got Palmer in the chest and knocked him sideways. Palmer's gun fired wildly. The shot ripped into another nitrogen pipe

123

behind Walker and the tiny hole expanded, blew outward in a stream of freezing liquid.

Walker went after Palmer, stunned him with a kick. Without a thought, he gripped the man's head and forced it into the cloud of foaming, surging white.

Palmer screamed in excruciating pain and his skin and muscle froze. His gun fell from his nerveless hand, clattered to the floor—

It seemed to be forever before Palmer's legs spasmed and twitched. He staggered out of Walker's grip, head and shoulders translucent white, and fell against the rail.

Walker didn't stop. He sent a spin-kick at Palmer's torso. The frozen man flipped over the rail—

—and fell to the concrete, where his head and upper body shattered like a cheap vase. A tide of frozen flesh and bone rolled across the floor in chunks and shards.

Jesus!

Walker turned. The senator had reached the top of the stairs. He looked down at his broken bodyguard. He seemed only slightly stunned from the electric shock. McComb's tracking module and Palmer's gun lay on the metal walk in between them.

Walker, exhausted and cold, managed an ironic smile. He tilted his head at what was left of Palmer. "Now *that's* when you say, 'freeze,'" he said.

McComb nodded slightly and moved casually forward. Walker saw the tension build behind his eyes.

"He got the idea," McComb said mildly, and moved closer. "Do me a favor—don't give up without a fight."

"It never crossed my mind," said Walker. All right. If he had to defend himself and McComb went over the railing, then so be it.

McComb's stare flickered, and Walker knew, didn't have time to turn.

A hand reached out and grabbed him by the shoulder, twisted him around—

Fielding punched him in the face, once, twice—he blocked and backed away from a kick. The tip of her boot snagged his chest, forced him back against the rail.

He slid into a defensive position, edged away as he held his arms up.

God, I hate this—

"I don't want to fight a woman," he said, and blocked another kick.

Behind Fielding, McComb rushed forward and grabbed for the chestpack and gun.

"Then *don't*," she spat.

The agent drove him farther down the walk with a set of kicks and punches. He blocked most of them, but took two hard hits to the chest and a glancing abrasion from her boot across his arm. He stayed covered, backed farther—

Fuck this, she's gonna beat the shit out of me!

So much for old-fashioned gallantry . . .

He reached out and caught her leg in mid-kick. "I changed my mind," he said, and then struck out with a solid kick to her ribs.

She reeled back. She clutched at him, pulled him around so that she was between him and McComb.

"Tell me he was gonna kill your family!" he yelled into her dazed face.

She turned, confused, and saw the senator with the chestpack and Palmer's gun, aimed in that direction.

McComb backed away from them. He fiddled with the control device.

Fielding realized what he was doing. She stumbled forward, hands hooked into pleading claws. "Don't you leave me, goddammit! Don't you dare—"

Over Fielding and the hiss of freezing air, Walker heard

sirens outside. The senator smiled, cold as the leaking nitrogen. "Don't you open that mouth to *me,* young lady," he said. Then he shot her.

He squeezed the trigger again and again. The rounds smacked into Fielding's chest and stomach. Blood sprayed until she was beyond screaming. The bullets drove her back; Walker, behind her, was shielded, even though McComb was trying to kill them both—

She kept backing away, trying to avoid the impact of the slugs. She fell into Walker, knocked him backward. He tumbled to the metal grate, her bloody, punctured body on top of him.

In spite of the deafening explosions lapping against the hard floor and walls, Walker heard the *click* as the automatic ran empty. McComb wasted no time—he dropped the useless weapon and stroked the controls on his chestpack.

Walker struggled to get out from under Fielding's dead weight—

"Adios, motherfucker! Stay here, Walker! In my future, you're dead!"

The flat plane of energy swirled into the clouded air, drew McComb inward. The machines and walls behind him wavered and sparked—

Walker heaved Fielding off, then leapt at McComb as the vortex swirled him away and into nothingness. He dove hard, but smashed into the empty walk.

McComb was gone.

The sirens were right outside. Walker heard doors slam, questions shouted. He couldn't stay to interact with the locals; it was against the rules. He had to move.

He slammed his hand against his own electronic pad and everything went away—

Sixteen

The first thing he heard when he came out of the jump was Matuzak's voice:

"Walker!"

The pod skid to a halt with a metallic screech. Smoke plumed up from the drag rockets and tailhook.

He was back in the launch bay, sans Fielding.

He popped the restraints and jumped out. Adrenaline surged through him, and he turned to find Matuzak, had to tell him—

He got two steps before he noticed what was happening.

A group of people he had never seen before rushed back and forth. They wore FBI vests and harried expressions. Walker stopped in his tracks and looked around. Boxed equipment, dismantled and labeled, towered around the launch tracks. One of the FBIs stacked chairs while two others ran inventory—

Matuzak hurried out from behind the protective blast barrier and joined Walker on deck. He looked . . . different somehow. More harried.

Walker's mouth went dry. He swallowed. "What the hell is going *on*?"

"You're lucky you got back, that's what— They're getting ready to tear up the tracks. I'd hate to go out on a sour note, losing one of my field agents. Even you."

Walker could barely hear, his already ringing ears not able to compete with the din of machinery and movement. But Mat's tone of voice didn't sound as if losing him before the tracks were ripped up would have been such a great loss.

Matuzak motioned for Walker to follow him to the gate.

They walked into the mostly empty corridor and toward launch control. The techs who buzzed past seemed lost in their own worlds, heads down. Walker was in a state of shock; he was hurt and dazed, and now the FBI—?

He looked over at Matuzak; the man's face was stern; angry, but resigned.

"McComb?" said Walker.

"Who else?"

Walker frowned. "But he hasn't got the authority—"

Matuzak raised his eyebrows. "You kiddin'? He's way out front in the polls, everyone knows he's got the election sewn up, it's a formality. You *knew* the committee was gonna cave, they don't want to get on the bad side of their new boss—"

Walker stopped and stared at Mat.

The director looked back at him as if he had blown a fuse during the jump. "What? It's been headed this way for *months*. We all saw it coming."

Things fell into place, but slowly. "When I left, nothing was happening—" he started.

Matuzak eyed him cautiously.

"Hey, Walker!" somebody yelled.

He looked away from Mat to see Ricky MacDonald with a hand raised in greeting from his work station—but not the Ricky he had known from before the assignment.

A smooth, well-groomed professional with Ricky's features stood in front of them. He wore a suit and tie under the crisp lab coat; his hair was perfect. The tech packed a box of personals—coffee mug, potted plant . . .

A potted plant? Ricky?

. . . and not one nude picture in sight, either.

Ricky grinned. "When they tear up the launcher, maybe you can have the pod as a souvenir," he said. "Use it as an easy chair in front of your TV."

Same crappy sense of humor, despite the new look—

Walker realized that all of the equipment in the room wore a different label—"Parker Datalink" had been replaced with one word: "McComb."

". . . *his* future—" he said, understanding what McComb had said, a few minutes—and a few *years*—back.

Holy shit. The senator had rescaled time. So this was what happened when somebody altered the past.

Just like in the theoretical scenarios.

It wasn't the same world Walker had left.

Matuzak moved a few steps away, out of Ricky's earshot. He tilted his head at Walker. "What're you talking about?"

More techs and FBIs carted equipment out of the control room and the revised Ricky hauled his box out with him.

No, this isn't happening—

He turned to Matuzak and pitched his voice low. "It's McComb. He's buying the presidency."

The chief snorted. "So what's new? Probably every President since Teddy Roosevelt has done the same thing."

"This guy has *killed* people."

"Wouldn't surprise me; he killed my agency."

Walker got impatient, leaned in. "*Hey*—he shot two people! I watched him do it. He would have killed me, too. He's crazy."

Matuzak stopped joking, peered closely at Walker. "Who did he shoot?"

Finally. "A man named Parker, Jack Parker—and Fielding."

"Jesus. I forgot all about her. You lost an IA agent?"

"*You* sent her with me. McComb blasted her."

"Sorry. Look, I don't like McComb one fuckin' bit, but just who do you think I could sell this story to? Without a smoking gun and fifty witnesses?"

"How about one witness?"

He scowled. "You don't count."

Walker looked away for a second, frustrated. Everything was different now, how could he make him understand—?

"Fielding." He grasped at it. "Maybe she's still alive. The local cops were there—"

Matuzak cut him off. "I'm gonna be looking for a new job next week, Agent Walker, and I doubt it'd help my chances much if I'm trying to put our next President in *jail*. Plus, McComb's enemies have a way of vanishing mysteriously."

"You think I'm making this up?"

"Forget it. It's too late. You're not going back. You can't."

"Look, if she's *alive,* we got him!"

Matuzak shook his head. "Don't you get it? We're *shut down.* As in history. We couldn't open a window now if we wanted, the equipment is *gone.*"

Walker took a deep breath. *Okay, this isn't gonna be easy—* He gritted his teeth and spoke clearly. "Come on, I want to show you something."

Matuzak sighed and allowed himself to be led to the squad room.

Half an hour later, Walker sat at the only operating terminal, with Matuzak next to him. The squad room was deserted and dismantled, most of the TEC officers packed and gone. *Oh, man.*

He had explained as much as he could, as well as he could. Now he just had to back it all up—

"These files are sealed," Matuzak said for the third time. "Now—*why* the hell am I doing this? Because we're best friends, is that what you said?"

Walker concentrated on the monitor. The confidential files were a bitch to get into; the code was fifty digits long, one error and you had to reenter it—

Got it.

He typed in "Fielding, Sarah" and waited while the system searched. He answered Matuzak's question. "For a long time."

Matuzak was still confused, but Walker could see the man's instincts surface along with his humor. "You say I *liked* you?"

Walker nodded.

"What are you looking for specifically?"

Walker looked back at the screen. "Any sign of Fielding—friends, relatives, anyone she could go to in 1994, if she survived."

The monitor flickered and then ended its search: "ACCESS DENIED."

He asked for a confirmation and got the same response. The FBI had shut down their system; they couldn't get into their own database anymore. *Damn.*

"She sold out, you said. So good riddance. She was IA, a headhunter; I won't lose any sleep over her, probably nobody will. Instant karma."

"Yeah. She had a deal with McComb . . ." He looked up blankly at Mat. "Look—we gotta go back and make sure she's dead."

"So run check the phone listings. If she's still alive, you

can give her a call, hash over all your good times back in '94. Do it on the government's nickel before they pull that plug, too—"

"This isn't funny. Two of us might be able to convince a judge."

"*If* she would talk to you. *If* she wasn't killed. *If* the judge didn't think you were making it all up to get back at the man who eliminated your job. *If*—"

"Christ, Mat, you've got to help me!"

Matuzak stared at him. "Because you say we're close friends, I'm gonna ask a question that I'm sure the prison shrink will ask you—" He lowered his voice. "How is our leading presidential candidate making these expeditions into the past without equipment, ol' pal o' mine? Time travel isn't something you whip up in an old mayonnaise jar in the basement. He's not using ours and he hasn't been jaunting all over the world to use anybody else's, either. Hasn't been to Japan, Iran, New Zealand, China, nowhere they've got the technology. He's been right here in the States running for President."

His tone was light, but Walker could see that Mat wanted to believe him.

If he could only give him a *reason* to believe.

He searched for an answer . . . "What about the prototype?" he said quietly. "It was never dismantled . . ."

Matuzak nodded. "Kleindast's . . . it's in Maryland, in Calverton."

Walker felt a rush of relief. Mat was still there, still a good cop in the face of a totally different reality; McComb had never gotten to him.

"It's only a short drive from Washington . . ."

Matuzak bit his lip. "Even if you're right, we've got no authority and we sure as hell can't just stroll into the place . . ."

"Ricky could get us in."

He shook his head.

A few seconds went past; they seemed like hours to Walker.

The cop won out over the bureaucrat. Mat pulled his keys out of his pocket. "If you were *really* my best friend, you wouldn't do this to me."

Walker turned off the system. Stood.

Maybe they'd be able to catch Ricky before he left the building.

It was the only shot they had.

And it was just the way Mat said, real goddamned iffy.

Seventeen

McComb told the story, enjoying it, then nestled back into the plush limo seat and brushed the salt off of a peanut. He held the crystal bowl on the tips of his fingers and smiled at Lawrence as he chewed.

The aide still wore several small white bandages across his face and head, and looked as if he might explode into a frenzy of nervous terror any second. In fact, he hadn't said a word since they'd pulled away from the Capitol—just made cooing sounds of agreement as the bright D.C. day rushed by.

McComb shrugged. "So I'd have him killed here and now, but if he's back, Matuzak knows. And God *knows* who else might have heard his story . . . Of course, they won't know what the hell he's talking about—but they'd give it a lot of thought if he turns up dead. A complication I don't need just now."

Lawrence nodded obediently as McComb ate another nut. "Right."

McComb sighed. "So, he has to be erased."

"Erased," Lawrence echoed, and nodded again, gaze stuck on McComb's hands, his every twitch.

Too bad Palmer's not here—

At least Palmer had a fucking clue; McComb didn't have to *explain* so much . . .

"We have to kill him *before* he was with TEC. Then nobody in the agency ever knew him or talked to him. I think."

"Perfect." Lawrence's face twisted into a sick expression, as if McComb had just spoken the word of God, but that of an angry God.

McComb leaned forward suddenly and shouted in the man's face. "It's *not* perfect, but it's what we got! And please don't think you're gonna be my chief of staff if slammin' your head into a car window turns you into a fucking sniveling *worm*!"

Lawrence sat perfectly still, eyelids squeezed shut. His complexion matched the Band-Aids on his sheep's face.

I am going to smite *you, Lawrence—*

Stupid.

McComb settled back into his seat again and smiled sadly at the aide. Replacement time soon, the poor man.

In a burst of generosity, McComb held the bowl of nuts out to him.

Lawrence finally moved, to flinch back from the offer.

The senator rolled his eyes and sighed. Disgusting, really.

He ate another peanut and thought about Walker.

Walker felt like shit. His entire body was a mass of aches and bruises, and he hadn't had a decent meal in days, not to mention any real sleep.

He and Matuzak stood behind Ricky's computer in the control room and watched him work. Walker was aware that he didn't smell too good, either, but no one else seemed to notice—actually, he didn't particularly give a shit himself, given all that had happened—

"There."

He leaned in closer to look at where Ricky pointed. There were still a few people around, but for the most part, the three of them had been ignored.

An electric power–demand graph was on the monitor, with several large spikes logged.

Ricky had his finger on one of the power surges. "At random intervals, Maryland Utility shows spikes in demand and duration that are almost identical to ours."

Walker couldn't have been readier. He looked at Matuzak. "See? You have to send me back. I'm right. You know I'm right."

Ricky sighed without looking back at them and spoke in his new by-the-book tone. "They won't let us do that," he started.

"Stay out of it, Ricky," said Walker.

"Say, would it be too much trouble to call me Richard?" The tech half turned in their direction.

Matuzak smiled at him. "Richard . . . do I have a best friend around here?"

Ricky shrugged. "It's not me. Gordon, I guess."

Matuzak nodded thoughtfully and glanced at Walker.

"Thanks, Richard," said Matuzak, and without another word, they left Ricky at his console and started for the launch facility.

They headed for the blast doors, side by side. Walker felt his adrenaline pump; Mat was gonna let him jump, whatever Ricky had said . . .

Matuzak spoke quietly as they marched down the deserted corridor. "Gordon is a putz. I can remember my best friend in the Marines, and my best friend as a cop—but Gordon isn't anything like either of them. I'm not saying you're right—but I want to see McComb take a big fall, so I'm gonna give you the benefit of the doubt."

Matuzak shook his head and snorted under his breath as they neared the facility. "*Gordon?* Come on."

There were two of McComb's men stationed at the blast doors. They were armed and bored, and both of them tensed as Mat and Walker got closer.

Walker let Mat do the talking.

One of the guards fingered his rifle and scowled at them. "Where are you going?"

Matuzak looked irritated. "We're venting the fuel shunts."

The guard looked at his partner and raised his eyebrows. The man shrugged.

The first guy looked back at them. "Is that right? Uh—you'll have to wait while I get authorization . . ."

The man reached for his vest com, and Walker moved. He stepped in, brought both arms up, and locked them. His hands pinched each of their throats, and he slammed them backward.

Each of the men cracked his head back into the heavy door. Then the only sound was the tiny gurgle out of the first guard's slack mouth as he hit the floor next to his buddy.

Two outs, bottom of the ninth . . .

Walker punched his security code into the wall panel; still valid. He shoved the door open and stepped past the unconscious men.

Matuzak shook his head, hesitated. He stared at the guards, then looked at the younger man and smiled ironically.

"Was I your *only* friend?"

Walker laughed softly in spite of the tension; he was going back.

Some of the machines were still on, and the secondary tracks hadn't been lifted yet. Despite what Mat had said earlier, they were still operational, but just barely.

They blocked the door and got to work. The room was clear, at least—although even if it had been jammed full with a dance party, Matuzak figured Walker could and *would* have taken them all out.

He watched as this virtual stranger belted into the pod. He and Walker, friends? Matuzak knew that the man's wife or girlfriend had been killed a long time back—it was in the file—but he never talked to *anybody*—

But he was committed, and somehow Mat could see that Walker was sincere about all of this; the Walker he'd known wasn't an open man, and he doubted that openness could be faked this well.

Friend or no, Matuzak didn't want to see Walker *die*. This was fucking dangerous, a jump without the tech crew . . .

He handed Walker a rope that he had strung to the chock-block beneath the wheel, and shouted to him over the noise machines.

"A launch isn't a one-man operation!"

Walker checked his panel and started to breathe deeply. "I know!"

"If I'm off on velocity or trajectory, you're gonna be an omelet!"

"You tryin' to scare me?"

Matuzak shot a look at the doors; they weren't going to have much time, once the engines started up—

"Yeah, I'm trying to scare you!"

He grinned tightly. "Just hit the right year!"

Eugene Matuzak was suddenly sure that he would never see his agent again. He opened his mouth to say something, but then closed it; in any reality, such a thought would have no impact on Max Walker.

"Good luck," he called out, and turned to walk away.

Walker reached out and grabbed Matuzak lightly by the arm. The surprised commander looked at him.

Mat looked straight into his eyes. "I've had your wife's Hungarian stew a hundred times," Walker said. "Always too much salt."

Matuzak grinned as he caught Walker's hand. They gripped firmly, warmly, and Walker wished that they had more time.

Without another word, they broke the grip.

Matuzak hurried down the tunnel to the launch controls.

Walker closed the pod's hatch.

The chief jogged across the track and started the sequence with the touch of a few buttons. The pylons at the far end started to spark and glow. Walker knew his boss had directed the jumps for a long time, he was hands-on. Any one tech wouldn't be able to pull it off, not with half the equipment gone, but Mat had overseen every aspect, and if anybody could, he would be the one . . .

Mat threw the switch for the rockets, and winced at the incredible noise.

"There goes my pension!" he yelled.

Walker tried to reach the Calm, but there was too much in his head and no time. McComb's goon squad would be on its way. From his belted-in position, he could see Mat at the power grid and only part of the blast doors.

When they got here, he wasn't going to be able to help Matuzak. He wished he had been able to say more to the man; he owed him one, big-time—

An automated voice crackled over the com. "Nine . . . eight . . . seven . . ."

The entry to the launch pad crashed in, and one of McComb's troops, a wormy man, pointed a weapon at Matuzak. Other armed men poured in behind him, stumbled over the fallen door guards. Headed for the pod.

Walker could hear it all: "Shut it down, *now*!"

Matuzak reached for a switch and pulled it. The automated voice called out again. "Polarity achieved. Five . . . four . . ."

The wormy man aimed. "Last chance!"

Matuzak calmly slapped down the last switch.

"Two . . ."

The Worm opened fire. The other guards were on the tracks, and bullets smacked into Mat's head and chest as another man pushed buttons, tried to stop it—

Matuzak died.

Walker screamed and pulled the rope. Flames erupted up the sides of the now-unprotected tracks—they'd taken out most of the shielding—and immolated the running guards. Cooked them into burned toast.

Good.

I'm sorry, Mat . . .

The G-force slapped Walker into his seat; his scream stretched and he headed for the plane of energy—

Time.

Maybe his last trip.

Maybe the last thing he would ever do.

He thought about the Vollmers.

Eighteen

Walker stood, dazed, a long-ago scream dead on his lips. He was in the middle of a road—

A blast of noise and pain thundered in his ears.

He spun and his jaw dropped.

"Shhiiiiit—!"

He fell to the hot pavement, heart about to explode. He kept his eyes glued open and watched as the eighteen-wheeler roared *over* him, doing eighty.

At least eighty—

He had "jumped" to the middle of the street several meters in front of a massive Peterbilt semi. A half second slower and he'd have been another bug splattered on the truck's grill. A real big gooey bug.

Then the truck was gone, headed down the highway.

Sun blasted his face, and a rush of turbulence ruffled his hair.

The asphalt seemed to sizzle beneath his back. He got to his feet. His knees shook.

"Shit," he said again, and started to walk.

• • •

He balanced the receiver of the pay phone against his ear and activated his chestpack's computer. He was in D.C. And the date was close—Mat had done a good job . . .

And suddenly he realized:

It was the last day of Melissa's life, the day after Fielding had been shot. Why hadn't he noticed that before, the last time he'd jumped?

He tried to put it out of his mind, but he couldn't, now that everything was different—

The phone he'd found was in front of a grimy 7-Eleven. He spoke quietly to the tiny computer.

"Access police mainframe. Victim Jane Doe, multiple gunshot wounds, McComb & Parker factory building—"

He fed in the essentials and waited, gnawed at his lip as the computer beeped to the telephone, dialed directly to the mainframe.

A young black kid walked out of the store carrying a soda the size of a tanker and raised his eyebrows, then moved on. Just another white guy with a computer on the phone. BFD.

Walker watched the screen as the computer searched, then stopped. An admission form filled the small screen.

Jane Doe/four gunshot wounds/admitted Wash. Med Center-Emergency 1600 hrs/ICU #2U.

Walker tapped the keys and shut down, a small smile of relief on his face. Sarah Fielding was still alive.

And so is 'Lis—

Walker shook his head and called a cab.

He walked into Washington Memorial and headed for Fielding's room; Memorial was where their doctor had worked. Melissa had taken him here the time he had

144

sprained his knee on a run, and they had sat in the emergency room for forty-five minutes . . .

The shades were down in the critical ward, the only sounds those of medical equipment—the hiss of an oxygen pump, the chirps and clicks of a heart monitor.

He had to get the nurses elsewhere, so he went into the bathroom down the hall and started a small fire in the wastebasket. By the time the smoke alarm went off, he was back outside ICU. The blare of the alarm brought nurses with extinguishers out of the unit. In the confusion, Walker slipped into the place and entered Fielding's room. He let the door slip closed behind him.

Fielding was alone. An IV hooked her to the single bed, and the stench of hospital disinfectant rushed over him.

He moved over to crouch beside her and felt a stir of pity at her pale face.

"Hey, happy birthday," he whispered.

Her eyes flickered open. She looked at him for a second before recognition flashed in her clouded gaze. ". . . Thanks," she murmured weakly. "Get me anything?"

"Tell me what you want."

She suddenly looked childishly small and hopeful in her bed. "I wanna go home," she said softly. She smiled, then added, "I already know who's gonna win the next ten world series." Her words were slurred.

He smiled back. Surprisingly, he felt no real malice toward the woman. "No problem."

"Why'd you come back?" she asked, eyes closed again.

No time to paint pictures. "I want you to testify against Senator McComb."

A frown of pain creased her brow. "It would be my pleasure."

He nodded. "It could be dangerous . . ."

"You mean I might get shot or something?"

He gave her a small grin. "McComb has already made changes. He's more powerful than he was."

She looked at him.

He sighed. "I've got to move fast. If I can find you, so can the bad guys."

She nodded weakly.

He continued. "I need positive proof that you were here, to back up our story—"

She smiled weakly. ". . . Just in case I don't make the trip? It's okay . . . They just took some blood, lab's down the hall I think . . ."

He stood. "Okay. Be right back." He reached for the door handle.

Fielding called out quietly from her bed. "Hey—"

He stopped and turned. She struggled to raise her head and look at him.

"I really screwed up," she said.

"Yes, you did."

"I want to make things right," she said, and then fell back into bed. He turned back to the door and she found some more air and added, ". . . Maybe you can make things right for yourself . . ."

He felt his gut clench at the thought, at that impossible thought—

"Be right back," he said again, and escaped into the hall.

The ICU lab was across from Fielding's room and down a few doors. Walker strolled past it, glanced inside, and then walked back and into the place. It was empty. Nothing like a little wastebasket fire to stir people along.

There was a tray of tubes on the generic counter, along with a stack of charts. Walker worked quickly; there was Fielding's printout and sample. He started to turn back to the door, gaze still on the tubes—

Walker, M.

Walker started to shake. No, it was impossible. The coincidence, it was *crazy,* not possible—

The sticker on the tray was hand-lettered. *Walker, M.* He reached out to touch it. He felt a wave of emotional pressure unlike anything he'd ever experienced before. Ten years ago, and he was here. It had been ten lonely, bitter years, and he had sworn allegiance to the agency, sworn to stay clean—and now this.

The inscription was brief:

Walker, Melissa. The house's address and their phone number. The date. And the result.

Pregnancy positive.

Nineteen

Walker rushed back into Fielding's room, still stunned. He ran over to her bed to tell her, that she'd been right, maybe he *could* change it—

"I'm gonna take you over to St. Paul, you'll be okay there! Listen, then I—I found something, I—"

A low, long, beeping noise filled the room, punctuated by a shrill squealing sound. Walker spun and looked—

Flatline.

He leaned over her bed and searched her placid face. "Hey, come on, we're getting you out of here."

There was a syringe jammed into her IV tube that hadn't been there two minutes before.

Fielding was dead.

"What are you doing?!"

An alarmed nurse stood in the doorway. She started toward him, then spotted the syringe. Panic flashed across her face, and she backed up quickly, into the corridor.

"Security! Somebody get Security here, stat!"

Walker ran to the door and past the shrieking nurse. Dammit!

He started down the hall at a run, toward the stairs—

And saw two men step into one of the elevators at the break in the hall, near the nurses' station. They were long coats, grim faces. And he would have recognized them anywhere.

The shotgunners. They had murdered Melissa, ten years ago. Today. And now Fielding—

He broke into a sprint, reached the elevator just in time for it to close in his face. The two men were gone.

He slammed his hands on the doors frantically and started to pull—

"Hey! Hey, don't move!"

He spun and saw two security guards hurrying toward him, followed closely by two more. "Hey!"

He gritted his teeth in frustration. "I'm a cop!" he shouted, and by the looks on their faces, he realized that they were going to keep him there awhile, time he didn't have, because it had dawned on him that the attack on Melissa was part of this, and if it was, then he had the right to go and save her.

He turned and ran down the continuing hall. Patients and staff members fell out of his path, the guards right behind—

There was an open door at the end of the corridor, and he ran faster. Corner of the building, next to the hedges, third- or fourth-level ledge. There was no way he could circle back to a stairwell or the elevators—

Christ, sixth floor, too—

He leapt through the room, past an old man in bed being visited by his kids, and threw himself out of the window. He aimed at what he prayed was a soft spot. Shards of glittering glass followed him down, down, down . . .

Thump! He landed feet-first on the fourth floor of the hospital, the top of the cafeteria. He let his knees go to avoid breaking both ankles. He crumpled down, rolled as he'd been taught in parasailing, then jerked himself up and ran to the edge. Patients and nurses ran to the Plexiglas walls to look out at him.

Below him was another angled level, two more stories down. Past that, the Emergency entrance, surrounded by a cluster of hedges and trees. He looked up. The security guards had stopped at the window; one of them shouted into his radio, called for more help—

He hoped that those trees would be gentle. He looked at the next drop, took a deep breath, and jumped—

Walker got to the downtown mall drenched with sweat and out of breath. It was warm and humid out, the blue sky cloudless . . .

"I think it's going to rain this afternoon."

God. Oh, Jesus. He had replayed this day so many times, the images were burned into his mind, and here it was, all of it. The new car display, the bright colors of the passing shoppers, the packed parking lot—even the smells were the same, fried foods and motor oil and the sticky air of early fall.

He felt as if he were going insane. He forced his aching legs to move.

He hurried into the mall and desperately scanned the crowd. His watch was broken, he must have hit it on something, but he didn't think it was quite noon yet.

He saw the mall pharmacy sign and started toward it. The package she had carried today, ten years ago—it had been lost in the fire, but if 'Lis had been pregnant, it would have held vitamins or prenatal drugs—

For the baby. Our unborn child.

Walker felt a rush of emotions that he couldn't begin to define—love, pride, joy, and pain. For what they had lost, and what might be gained . . .

151

And your job, Walker, what about the job?

If the two men at the hospital were involved, it was a time discrepancy, one the TEC hadn't caught. And that meant that it was his *job* to make things right again.

Either way, he was going to try and save her. There had been too many coincidences today for him to disregard. It was his destiny, or at least it seemed to be—and if that was a rationalization, so be it.

As in "Fuck it." All bets were off.

Walker thought these things in a few seconds as he moved toward the drugstore. A blare of noise snapped him back to the moment, coupled with an obnoxious, heavy bass line.

Skates, the kid on in-line skates. He jerked his head around to see the young gangbanger approaching. His radio blared, and he actively ignored the irritated glances from the shoppers forced to get out of his way.

He waited until the punk was almost next to him, then lashed out with a solid side-kick. He caught the kid at thigh level. The surprised Skates crashed through the open door of a mall shop and fell into a pottery display. Shards of broken ceramics flew. The radio fizzled out in mid-screech.

Skates turned a shocked, pimply face up to Walker. Guilt already lurked behind his sullen eyes.

"That's for what you're going to do," said Walker, then hurried on. Time was malleable but not here and now: Now it was all too short.

He was almost there. He anxiously scanned the moving crowd, and then felt his heart stall dead in his chest.

She walked out of the drugstore, a dreamy, unfocused look across her delicate features. Melissa, more beautiful than his faded memories could ever recall. There was a glow about her that he hadn't remembered, something that he saw and understood now.

He wanted nothing more than to scream out her name, run to her and take her far away. He opened his mouth—and stopped in his tracks. He reached up and touched the scar that twisted across his temple.

He didn't want to scare her; he watched as she walked across the crowded corridor, package gripped in one lovely hand. She moved to stand in front of the antique clock store, where he had found her so long ago—

Only Walker realized now that she hadn't been watching the time that day after all; there was a maternity shop adjacent to the clock store, filled with tiny dresses and jumpsuits aflash with primary and pastel colors.

As he watched, heart full, she placed a hand across her stomach and smiled. It was eight minutes until twelve. He was early, here before his younger self would arrive. He had to hurry.

He started toward her, then stopped again. His eyes narrowed, his instincts sharp and alarmed. The two men from the hospital, from Melissa's dying moments, walked past, headed for the drugstore.

They didn't see him, and he didn't dare follow . . .

Seven minutes. He moved up to stand behind Melissa, his emotions barely in check. Behind her, he studied her face in the window, then saw his own appear and sharpen. Older, much older, but perhaps she would listen first—

He cleared his throat and found that it was choked with fear. He spoke timidly, carefully, replayed the conversation from painful memory.

"There's never enough time—"

Her eyes brightened, her lips touched by a casual smile. "Never enough for what?"

He swallowed hard. She started to turn, but he wrapped his arms around her and squeezed, as gently as he could manage. "A woman," he whispered.

His wife arched one eyebrow. Had she done that before, was this right—?

"Then you never want to miss an opportunity," she said. Her light perfume filled his senses, the touch of her skin—

He struggled to manage the words, whispered, ". . . Are you busy?"

Her face was playfully deadpan. "I'm meeting my husband."

He couldn't breathe. He wasn't going to be able to do this, not without breaking apart—

She continued, but mild anxiety flashed across her brow as she studied his reflection. The words weren't exactly the same now; close, but not precisely as he recalled: "I didn't hear you—uh, leave this morning . . ."

He kept his arms around her, tight. All he wanted was this; it was all he had ever cared about. She tried to turn again.

"No, 'Lis, don't turn around yet—"

The anxiety changed to worry. "What's the matter?" The tenderness in her voice made him weak. "What's wrong?"

He couldn't stop her. With an effort, she twisted in his grasp to face him.

The fear on her face stabbed his heart. She pulled back, bumped against the glass front of the clock shop and dropped the pharmacy bag.

"It's all right," he said, and held his hands out to her. "Listen—"

"Who are you?" Her voice was strained and confused, loud.

He reached out and took her shaking hands. He moved them up to rest on his face, creased and wrinkled with lines she didn't know.

"It's me, Max," he said softly, and saw that she was

trying. Her fingers traced his brow, stopped at the faded scar—

"What happened to you? Max . . . ? It is you, isn't it? But changed . . ."

People had stopped to look; a frightened woman being confronted by a large stranger—

He glanced at the pharmacy. The two men stood in front of it, looked around. And spotted them.

He talked fast. "I'll tell you, but not here. Please, 'Lis, this is important. It's *me*."

She nodded weakly. Whatever else she thought, she knew him.

"Come on, we have to get out of here." The two men had started toward them.

Melissa hesitated. Five minutes left.

He took her arm, and she allowed herself to be led away, dazed by his appearance. They hurried down the main concourse toward someplace quieter, Walker's heart in his throat.

He risked a look over his shoulder before they turned into an empty service alcove; the two men had split up, and one of them moved slowly toward them. His cruel eyes searched the crowd patiently.

Walker shoved his stunned wife through a door marked "Delivery Access" and prayed that the killer didn't see them. With each passing second, he could feel his only real happiness tick toward destruction. He could only hope that there was a chance, that fate would be kind and let him save his family.

Family.

Dear Lord in heaven. His family.

Twenty

It was a back delivery entrance for some of the smaller stores. Walker led Melissa past stacks of empty boxes and overflowing trash bins and searched for a way out. Whether or not the man or men had seen them duck in here, they'd figure it out pretty fast.

The hallway turned left up ahead, maybe thirty meters. He pulled her along, strained his ears for the sound of the door opening . . .

She stopped and jerked her arm out of his grasp before he could stop her. He saw an expression on her face that he had almost forgotten—his heart twisted in his chest.

She wore the same look she had worn when he had wanted a new Magna 1100 motorcycle or the time he had tried to talk her into skydiving. Lower lip out, eyes narrowed, brows arched high. Melissa Taillefer Walker was not going one more step.

"Stop!" She ran one hand through her brilliant hair. "I want to stop, please! Tell me what happened to you!"

He glanced at the door back to the mall and bit at his lip.

"'Lis, it won't be easy, but try and believe me. I love you. You have to trust me—"

He raised one finger to his mouth as the door to the mall clicked. The latch was being turned, very slowly. He reached for her hand and led her to one side of the hall. One of the entrances to a storage area stood partway open. It was a back room to one of the mall stores, littered with shelves of boxes and circuitry. He pulled her inside and closed the door gently.

Melissa stared intently up at him, looked for her husband in his eyes. Her gaze wandered back to the scar on his forehead. Walker could see her analytical mind processing new information.

"You're not Max," she said, but with no real force. "You can't be."

No time. "Yes, I am. Ten years from now."

He wished he could explain first, to cushion her as much as he could. But as she peered closer, he saw in her eyes that she wouldn't rule it out.

"That's not possible . . ."

He stared back into her, hoped that she would be able to see past ten years of life without her, to the Max she knew.

"Matuzak. The new job, more hours, more risk, same pay—we . . ." God, it sounded so improbable! "We police time."

Melissa's eyes widened. He had told her too much too fast, but there was no way around it.

"*Time* travel?" She smiled, frightened and trying to cover it. "Umm, please, don't try to tell me this . . ."

He laid gentle hands on her shoulders. "TEC—Time Enforcement Commission."

He watched her turn it over, the brightness of her eyes, and suddenly he wondered why she had ever married a man like him. He couldn't stop a small smile of pure love for her.

158

"If I ever need a birdhouse built, I'll know who to see," he said.

"My God . . . I don't believe it—" But she did, he could see it.

"Try."

Melissa smiled hesitantly, tried to digest the strange truth. "What am I like ten years from now?"

He wouldn't let himself flinch, wouldn't scare her anymore, but it was one of the hardest things he'd ever done. "Just like now. Perfect."

He turned and pushed open the door to the inside of the shop. Perhaps another hint from destiny—they were in the room full of antique clocks.

The owner, a short, round man, stood in front of the store and watched the mess get cleared up from the Skates incident. They were alone, with a hundred clocks that bravely ticked away.

"You came back here—time-traveled—how? In what? Why? What is going on?"

Walker saw the clocks all turn to 11:59, and he turned and searched for the reason through the front window. He almost didn't recognize himself—

A young man with straight shoulders and a smooth brow was on the far side of the mall, walked happily toward them. He gestured at the man he barely remembered and looked at his wife. Their wife.

"Today is special. You have something you can't wait to tell him."

She stared out at her young husband, then back at him, as if he were a ghost. "How do you know?"

"I just told you."

"What are you here to prevent? What's going to happen?" 'Lis was openly anxious now.

He took a breath and said as much as he could. "Changes

159

in the past. I . . . It's going to be okay, really. I'll tell you later." He motioned again at her young husband as he strolled up the corridor. "Go meet him, and don't tell him anything about this, please. He doesn't need to know yet, and I'll be around in case anything . . . odd happens. But don't keep *your* secret, not for long. He really needs to know."

She turned and watched the young Max come closer. He wanted to say so much more, but the clocks were forced by nature to change. Suddenly the store was filled with an almost deafening series of chimes and buzzers; it was twelve o'clock.

Walker the elder reluctantly moved to the back of the store and slipped away.

He was too far away to hear what they said to each other, but he knew it all by heart. The impossibly younger version of himself pulled out his wallet and paid the photographer three dollars.

Their conversation echoed through his mind.—*you're going to be very happy you got this/what makes you think so*—

He pulled the tattered photograph from his own pocket, then looked over to where Melissa and Max Walker flirted, picture perfect. 'Lis was paler than she should have been . . .

"I can see into the future," said Walker, only there was no one there to hear him. He slid the photo back into his pocket and felt his eyes brim with thick tears; he would protect them as best he could.

The young couple joined hands and walked on.

Twenty-One

The young Senator McComb was late. Along with everything else, he had to meet with that asshole John, then put in an appearance at that stupid dinner for the retiring judge . . .

He banged through the doors of the Senate building, glared at his watch, and started for the stairwell. As long as he had sworn to lay off candy bars, he might as well take the stairs instead of the elevator.

The door to the stairwell almost slammed shut on the young aide who followed him. This one had the puppy-dog face of a recent graduate, probably ivy-league if you judged from the impeccably knotted tie.

McComb ignored him and started up the steps.

"Senator! Senator McComb, sir!"

Hell.

McComb turned. The aide anxiously held out a slip of folded paper.

"This was with the Senate operator, sir."

McComb tripped down the steps and snatched the message from the obsequious grad, who kept on.

"Sir? It's almost six-thirty. You've got a seven o'clock with—"

"Clear the rest of my schedule for tonight," McComb snapped. He crumpled the paper into his pocket. "All of it."

The look of surprise on the puppy's face would have been funny—except the message had just sucked the humor out of his day. McComb reached up and lightly touched the large bandage that quilted his cheek; it wasn't over yet . . .

McComb suddenly grabbed the aide's arm. "Have you ever been inside the President's limo?"

The puppy answered sincerely. "No, sir!"

He smiled briefly at the kid. "Keep in touch," he said. "I'll send you a picture."

He turned and pushed by the befuddled kid, in more of a hurry than he had been. He hurried through the lobby and out to where his limo waited, and once again reached up to stroke his wound.

That fuck was going to be sorry, very sorry he had ever crossed paths with Aaron McComb.

Walker kept his gaze on the car in front of them as the young couple went home.

The silent cabbie hung back a sufficient distance.

They got to the house in the early afternoon, and Walker paid the cab off and just watched the house for a while, remembering. He stood near the stand of trees at the front, patterned with shadows. Upstairs, he knew that a younger Max Walker would be making love to his wife. It had been a beautiful time, had touched him so deeply. When the rain started down, as evening swelled into dusk, he moved away from the tiny grove to stand in the soaked grass.

He looked up to their bedroom window and wondered if she had told him about the baby yet. He didn't remember—now, as an older Max—that she had, but with the Paradox,

162

maybe it would suddenly pop into his mind, just like that scar had appeared on McComb's face. Time travel was full of crap like that. It was enough to drive you crazy.

He was pretty sure she wouldn't have told him about the time stuff—it wouldn't have sounded sane, and he guessed she was probably more ready to believe it had all been her imagination. At the very least, she would chew on it for a while before she brought it up; that was how she'd always been. As of now, he didn't remember that she had told him about it, so she hadn't changed time by doing so. Yet, anyhow.

As for the baby, well, it was so hard to imagine, the mixture of emotions that the news would bring—would he have laughed, cried? Made love to her again? Or just held her and talked quietly about the future, their lives together . . .

His thoughts caught as he heard the light trill of his phone upstairs. It rang once, twice—if she had told him, he wouldn't answer, would he—?

The rings cut off, and a second later, the young Walker moved past the rain-swept window, receiver to his ear.

Both Walkers frowned—the young man on the phone because it was the office; the drenched outsider because it meant she hadn't said anything yet . . .

"Don't leave her, you fool," he whispered up to the house, and then he couldn't wait any longer. The killers would be coming soon.

He moved across the lawn to the front door.

The extra key was under the star-shaped rock beneath the hedge. He felt tears threaten again at the simple memory, then shook it off and let himself in. He was getting grainy, exhausted. Too much had happened. He wasn't tracking well, he wasn't in control. It was like a bad drug trip; life was bent and crooked, and he wasn't sure what was real and what was misperception.

163

He walked into their home, still feeling like a stranger with a fatal case of nostalgia, and waited.

Melissa, tousled beautifully from their time together, rushed into the room, didn't see him. Her robe hung open, and he felt the need to avert his eyes from her nakedness. He ran one cold, wet hand over the edge of their coffee table, her framed pictures—

Melissa stopped, startled. She cinched her robe tightly, surprised and frightened.

"You didn't tell him about the baby," he said.

She glanced up the stairs, but the young Max was still getting dressed. She walked closer toward him. He stood perfectly still, to avoid touching her.

"He didn't give me a chance," she said. "And as for you . . ."

"You didn't tell him about me, either. Good. But as for the other . . . you should've tried. . . ," he started.

Her mouth turned downward.

"You don't remember how much you loved being a cop?" she whispered, angry. "You always had it on your mind, it was uncomplicated, 'the Job'—"

"I remember," he said, his voice soft. He turned away again, to look out at the pouring rain. "I remember this rain . . ." 'Lis must have sensed something. Her voice became curious, hesitant.

"Are we still together? Ten years from now?"

He closed his eyes, listened to the rain patter down. "Yes," he said. "We're together."

She came closer, and he remembered how impossible it had been to keep anything from her. "Do you have a picture? One of us together? Or me?"

"Uh, no. Nothing recent."

"Oh . . . am I dead?"

Stunned, he looked up and met her gaze. He dropped his own. "No, you're not dead."

"What about tomorrow? That's why you're here, isn't it? Those men at the mall. They've come from your time. Why?"

He shouldn't have bothered; 'Lissa would know, as always. He met her brilliant stare again and his heart pounded.

"Don't ever let me leave you again," he said, and his love for her showed in the intensity of his voice; he couldn't stop it.

"What about the baby?" She was afraid, but in control.

"Everything's going to be okay," he said, hoped she would believe it. Hoped it was possible . . .

"Why can't we just get out of here? Can't we run from whatever it is?"

He looked at her and shook his head. "No. They'd come back, as many times as it takes. It has to end tonight."

Suddenly there were sounds over the rain, wet footsteps and low voices. A flashlight beam ran over the curtained living room window and disappeared.

Melissa started to back away.

He went to her, put his arms around her tightly. There was no way for him to explain himself any better, to calm her fears—

"You remember what happened here, don't you? It was bad, wasn't it? It was me, wasn't it? And the baby—?"

She stopped. "What makes you think it'll be different this time?" She whispered, and he could hear the terror there. There was nothing left to keep from her, she *knew*—

"Ten years alone," he said. He faced her, his voice stern. "And I'm here now; I wasn't before." He looked away for a moment, then back at her. "Keep him—keep *me* upstairs, whatever it takes." He dropped his hands to rest on her flat stomach, and something tugged at his heart like a barbed hook. "Tell him about the baby, now. That will do it. If he comes down here—"

'Lis stared up at him, as if she understood what would happen now.

"Go on!"

She turned and ran back up the stairs.

He stood for a second, glared helplessly at the front door. What could he do? They would wait for him to step outside, but he had an advantage now: He knew they were there.

He wasn't quite ready. He had to know something first.

He went to the stairs and crept silently toward their room. Their door was mostly closed, but he could hear them clearly.

". . . I want to tell you before you go." She was adamant.

"Can't it wait till I get back?" The young Walker sounded irritated and sorry at once. "It's only half a shift."

The older Walker pressed himself against the wall tighter, winced as his younger self tried to put her off. Had he been so *blind*?

Listen to her this time, please, please!

He edged forward until he could see, through the crack at the hinges of the door, a sliver of mirror. The young Walker straightened his tie, expression set.

Melissa's voice was painful to hear, her emotional restraint almost entirely gone. "*Max* . . . listen! I'm . . . I'm . . ."

He saw the young version of himself stop. His eyes seemed to bore into the mirror as he stared into the reflection of his wife's face. It hit him, like a fist to the gut:

"You're pregnant?" he whispered, awed. His hands dropped.

The old Walker felt a tear join the wetness of his coat as an enormous smile spread across his face. The young man

166

in the room wore the same expression. He disappeared from sight, and Walker the elder heard them come together. Melissa started to cry.

Well. I wasn't totally stupid back then. Back now.

He floated with the pain and joy for only a second, then took a deep breath and started back down the stairs. He cleared his mind as best he could as he headed for the front door, centered himself. Things had changed. He remembered it now, her telling him about the baby, that sudden jolt, the awe and joy of it. What happened right afterward was fuzzy in his memory—it happened, but it hadn't happened to *him* yet.

But he knew one thing for sure.

He was going to go out into the rain and kill the fuckers that had stalled his life—or at least hurt them so badly that they would wish they had never heard of Max Walker.

Time was precious and their time was *up*.

Twenty-Two

Walker tensed himself, then opened the front door and stepped outside.

The shotgun butt swung from the right at his head.

He pivoted to one side, reached out, and caught the stock. *Not this time, pal.* "Surprise," he said.

Shotgun stood, weapon gripped tightly, a shocked look of anger on his wet face.

"Who the fuck are you?"

"Friend of the family." Walker twisted and wrenched the weapon partway out of Shotgun's confused hands. The violence of the movement jerked at the trigger, discharged the gun—part of the porch exploded loudly into fragments of wood.

Walker snatched the gun away and hurled it off into the dark, then spun.

Shotgun raised his fists and snarled.

Walker didn't wait. He flew into the man, snapped a series of blows into Shotgun's stomach. At the same time, his right foot connected solidly with the man's crotch, three, four times. He was going to beat him to a fucking pulp.

Shotgun doubled over, tried to protect his crushed scrotum.

Walker smacked his hands away, kicked and punched in a rage. The final kick sent Shotgun over the porch rail to land in the wet grass. He landed on his back, didn't move.

Walker spun again as two dark shapes rushed into the faint halo of light from inside—the men he couldn't forget. The first held a pistol out—

He dove off the porch as bullets ripped the front door apart. He landed in the mud, shoulder-rolled up, and sprinted around the house, past the fallen Shotgun.

He stopped as soon as he was around the corner.

The rain poured down as he caught his breath. And listened.

Max Walker hugged his wife tightly, happier than he could ever remember being. A *baby* . . .

Fuck covering some guy's shift! This was where he belonged, with his family—

A baby! Our baby!

When he heard the first blast of gunfire, 'Lis started to cry louder, and he realized that she was almost hysterical. She clutched at him weakly.

Walker let her go and ran to the bedside table. He jerked the lower drawer open and pulled out his backup pistol, a small Glock, checked it—

"Max, no!" 'Lis tried to block the door, limbs trembling, as she pleaded openly. "Don't go down there, please! You can't!"

He looked at his terrified wife, confused—
What the fuck was going on?

Walker the elder shot a glance around the corner. The two killers had stopped by Shotgun, who rolled up into a

170

half-sitting position and groaned. One of the killers spoke angrily.

"How'd you miss?"

The moaning again as Shotgun clutched his testicles. "It's the TEC cop, he knew it was comin'!"

The second killer spat into the mud. "That son of a bitch doesn't know how to *die*."

The first shrugged. "He'll learn tonight." He reached down and picked up the wet shotgun, handed it to the fallen man. He then motioned toward the side of the house, where Walker waited.

"You don't kill him, you don't go back," he said simply.

The two killers went to the front door and inside.

Walker slipped away, around to the back of the house.

Through the back porch windows, he saw the two men in the living room. They carried flashlights, or had lights taped to their weapons, he couldn't tell which from where he stood—one of the killers started cautiously up the stairs, moved slowly. The light of the other one disappeared into the hallway toward the rec room.

And Shotgun would be coming for him—*shit*. He took one last glance at the light that moved up the steps inside and then edged back into the deeper shadows. If he'd been thinking clearer, he would have done it differently. He should have gone out the back door, circled around, blasted from behind. Should have.

He'd just have to hope that he remembered himself right as the young man upstairs—that the younger Max Walker would be able to protect Melissa, save her, now that he was alert and ready. And change both of their fates . . .

The stranger with the long coat and the flashlight taped to his pistol moved up the dark stairs slowly. He reached the top and crouched, aimed for their bedroom—

A flicker of hurried movement. The stained-glass window on the landing, at the far end—the panes of rainy glass were open and the gauzy curtains fluttered wildly.

From where he stood, the killer couldn't miss Melissa on the roof. She scrambled across the slick shingles toward the safety of an attic gable, wet and terrified—

The killer cased the upstairs rooms quickly and walked to the open window, a mean smile on his face. He parted the curtains and looked out at her.

She was on all fours, an easy target, soaked robe stuck to her legs. She looked over her shoulder, face white against the rainy dark, in time to see the killer move closer, take aim—

The killer forgot to look up.

Just step closer, you asshole—

Max watched the man take aim at his wife from overhead, confused and furious. He was suspended silently in the hallway above the killer, legs stretched across the width of the ceiling beams, gun holstered—

There!

The stranger moved closer to take better aim—

Max swung down and kicked hard.

The man went headfirst through the open window, the only sound his knees as they cracked against the sill.

Max dropped to the landing and saw the light from the man's weapon skitter across the shingles and fall into darkness.

What the *fuck*? There was another one somewhere, he was sure of it, but who? And why?

Who *were* these guys?

Walker anxiously peered out the window for Melissa.

She was huddled against the gable, a picture of misery. When he raised his hand and leaned out to call to her, her face changed, mouth fell open—

She screamed something that was almost lost in the thunder of rain.

"Max! *Look out!*"

He struggled to hear her, understood. Before he could react, reach for his gun, the killer lunged forward from nowhere—

—under the eaves—

—and grabbed him, wet claws against his arms.

The stained glass shattered, erupted around him as he rolled forward. His back slammed against the slippery roof and he rocketed down toward the edge.

Melissa screamed, and the sound forced him to act. He shot his hands out and grabbed for something, anything— the stranger who'd tried to kill him still clutched the exploded window.

His fingers found the rain gutter as he crashed over the second-story ledge, snatched at it. He got a solid grip, but when he tried to vault himself back to the roof, the old nails creaked and popped. The ancient gutter wasn't going to let him back up.

He hung there, helpless.

Melissa screamed again and again as the killer edged forward and started to kick at the loose gutter.

Shotgun slid along the back porch carefully. His breath came in short gasps, and every few meters, he stopped and winced painfully from his throbbing balls.

He nervously edged to the side of the house, heard what sounded like screams from the roof. His feet slipped and squelched in the mud, and the dark rain made it nearly impossible to see.

"Shit," he mumbled, and raised the shotgun to aim at nothing.

Lightning flashed; the bright sizzle cut through the

blackness somewhere close, thunder right behind. Shotgun looked up—

—and into Walker's eyes, in the window glass. The light was gone already, but he knew he had been seen. He bolted—

Shotgun fired into the kitchen. The blast shattered glass and wood, thundered louder than the night sky.

Shotgun ran to the next window. He caught another glimpse of Walker in the glass and pumped a round into the chamber. Another blast, furniture and wall blew into shreds, then another.

Shotgun ran to the third window and stopped. The pane was already cracked, shards gone. Walker's scarred face was a bizarre art piece, flickered closer with another burst of lightning—

Shotgun finally figured it out.

The panicked killer wheeled around; Walker had been outside all along, had run with him, *behind* him—

He flew into Shotgun, kicked the weapon away before he had time to point it—

Shotgun grabbed him with surprising strength and they fell to the mud.

He screamed in fury, wanted to tear Shotgun's heart out and take a bite. This man had tried to kill him, kill his beautiful *wife*—

They wrestled frantically as the sky rumbled and flashed over them.

'Lissa, no!

The killer stamped at his hands now, tried to dislodge his grip. Melissa, as angry now as terrified, left her position at the gable and stumbled toward them.

Max ignored the man's crushing kicks, the bones that

snapped in one shaking hand—Melissa ran, and crashed to the roof as the shingles slid out from under her feet.

She came down hard on one side and slid straight down, headed for where Max hung. He struggled to twist to one side, to stop her with his legs, but there was no way—

"Grab me!" he shouted.

She reached out—and slid right past, out and over the edge.

—*Baby*—

He shot one bloodied hand out and caught Melissa's wrist.

The sudden crunch of weight almost tore the gutter away from the house, and he scrabbled, supported them with one hand. 'Lis dangled precariously but held as still as possible, good girl—

Rusty water from the bent metal poured into his eyes; both his palms were wet with slime and blood, and he held on with everything he had left—

The killer's face hovered over them, grinned cruelly. "Nothing soft to land on?" He raised one heel, to crush the bones of Max's hand—

He felt his wife reach across him, as carefully as she could—

"Not yet, asshole," he said.

Suddenly the roof beneath the killer's feet exploded outward, dropped him.

Max held on as the killer took slugs to the legs and chest, screamed in shock and pain—and fell, plummeted past them to land with a sick *thud* on the wet ground.

Melissa had unholstered his pistol with her free hand, fired blindly, but well—

His grip was starting to give. He used the last of the strength of his shaking arm to raise them up a few centimeters, kick at the bullet-weakened overhang. A solid wooden beam jutted out—

He swung their weight over and hooked one leg over the beam. His clawed, frozen hand fell away from the tortured gutter.

She dropped the empty gun and grabbed his hand, their fingers intertwined.

He hung upside down and lowered her toward the ground. When she was only a couple of meters up, she let go, and dropped into the mud next to the dead or dying killer.

"*Run!*" he shouted, and she nodded, hair plastered to her skull. "Go on!"

'Lissa's eyes were full of pain and love as she screamed to be heard over the pounding rain. "I'll get help!"

She turned and disappeared into the dark. His prayers and hopes went with her; she was going to be okay, *had* to be okay.

He hauled himself up onto the roof and crawled across the shingles, back to the ruined window. He would find the other one. And kill him . . .

He had gripped the window frame tightly and started to climb through—

—when a light appeared at the top of the landing, and he found himself faced by the second killer. Who held a loaded pistol, aimed at his chest.

"Hey! Say, ahhhhhh!" Killer Two screamed, then fired twice.

The shots hit Max in the chest. He felt a brilliant flash of pain. His ribs snapped as he flew back out the window, hit the overhang—

The last thing he felt was the nails of the broken gutter ripping into his back before the ground, impossibly black, rushed at his face and smashed him into unconsciousness.

Twenty-Three

Shotgun tried to work his way closer to the fallen weapon, wriggled away through the mud like a demented snake as Walker kidney-punched him. Somewhere along the way, he had lost his gun. He couldn't have said where.

Shotgun shoved him away, hard, then crawled over him.

Walker's face was packed into the wet earth by the push, and he came up angrier, blinded by water and muck. Blood from a shallow head cut ran down and added to the problem.

He swiped the mud away and kicked upward at Shotgun's belly. The man gasped for air and struggled up to a crouch—

Shotgun dove for the weapon, Walker right behind. The man snatched up the barrel and yanked. Walker got a tenuous grip on the stock, and the weapon, wet and slick with the rain, slid in both their grasps.

Walker was on his feet. He tried desperately to get a better grip, but the damn thing kept *moving*—

Shotgun sat on the ground and tugged frantically; Walker was stronger than he was, he must've known it—he didn't stand a chance without a gun . . .

He didn't mean for it to happen, but in the struggle, Shotgun's hand slipped from the trigger guard. Shotgun had the muzzle stuck right in his crotch, point-blank, and Walker jerked, pulled—

Boom!

Walker caught the weapon as it fell out of Shotgun's surprised hands.

Shotgun looked down blankly at the smoking pit of his groin—where his dick once was, and now wasn't. Not a shred.

He looked up again. Rain spattered his face, and he opened his mouth, shocked into another reality—the blood gushed out and told how bad it was.

"That's gotta *hurt*—"

Walker couldn't find it in his heart to feel sorry for the asshole, even as said asshole toppled over into the mud and died.

More where that came from; he checked the shotgun. Empty. Of course. He didn't have time to look for ammo—no time, no time!

He left the gun next to the dead man's crumpled body and cautiously moved back toward the rear porch, aching and painfully awake, senses stoked. There had been other shots fired in the thundering dark, and he prayed that they had been aimed at the bad guys; he'd gladly kill every one of them if it meant Melissa and Max could go away . . .

Something banged loudly on the back porch. The kitchen lights were out, the shadows dense and sodden. The door was wide open; it thumped against the side of the house again, a prisoner of the wind.

He stepped onto the porch and edged for the banging door. Shotgun was down, that meant maybe two others.

He searched the darkness inside and suddenly a huge

weight slammed into his back. A big man crashed into him from behind, drove him into the kitchen.

He fell forward, then spun, but the killer had caught him off guard. He hit the wall just inside the door, the huge man pinned him—

"Cole!"

—and stopped. Walker tensed, looked at the attacker, Cole, then to where the voice had come from, a voice he *knew*—

The shadows at the far side of the dark kitchen shuddered, then reformed a few steps closer.

Three people. Another seedy flunky he hadn't seen before—

And Aaron McComb, the older version. With one manicured hand clamped securely over Melissa's mouth.

Her frightened eyes searched for his, and he felt a painful, horrible stab at his heart. McComb had 'Lis. Her slender, wet body quaked with terror and fury, pressed against McComb's side, and the bastard looked cool enough to be giving a speech at a fucking dinner.

Unless Walker thought of something fast, they were all going to die.

McComb held the woman tighter, gratified to see the hot fury on Walker's face.

Good. This little man, this . . . *shit*, had caused him a lot of trouble; McComb hoped that this was killing him. He wanted to see Walker twist in the breeze . . .

He smiled pleasantly at the old TEC officer and gripped Melissa's face hard enough to make her squeal a little. "Lousy night to be out," he said. Conversational.

Walker's expression was carefully blank, but his eyes were tortured, and when he spoke, his stupid accent cracked painfully.

"Don't hurt her . . ."

McComb nodded at Cole.

Cole slammed his fist solidly into Walker's gut, doubled the agent over in pain.

Cole straightened up and looked over to Reyes, McComb's newest "special assistant." "Cuff him."

Reyes stepped forward and grabbed Walker's wrists, twisted them up behind his back, cuffed him tightly. Cole moved back to flick on one of the small kitchen lights. The shadows scurried to the corners of the room.

This was better than McComb had hoped for! He waited, made certain that Walker was firmly in hand. Reyes and Cole flanked the cop.

McComb dragged the struggling woman across the dim kitchen to stand in front of Walker; he wanted them both to see all of it, each to experience the other's pain and fear—

The thought was giving him an erection.

He addressed the agent with an apologetic grin. "You know, you were at a disadvantage in this right from the beginning; you see, I'm an ambitious, Harvard-educated visionary—I *deserve* to be in power, it's my—my *birthright*."

McComb scowled at Walker's lack of interest. Was the man even listening? He just stared at his little wife, coldly oblivious to what McComb said.

"You," he spat out, "you're a fuckin' idiot who never figured it out. The only way to make anything out of yourself with all that fancy kicking is on *Broadway*."

The stupid frog didn't blink. "Thanks for clearing that up," he said.

McComb looked at Cole, who smiled widely and unloaded another massive punch to Walker's stomach.

Melissa Walker's lithe young body tensed and shook against the senator as the agent sagged forward again.

"Polls have me winning by twenty-eight points," Mc-Comb continued. It felt good to be in such control, a tiny taste of the future . . . "Biggest landslide since Nixon, way back in '72. It's reassuring to know what's going to happen, don't you think?"

He directed the last part to the woman as he pulled his little package out from his pocket. McComb glanced down at the digital readout; it was all set to go.

He tapped a button on the side of the bomb. The countdown clicked into motion.

"It's called C4," he whispered into Melissa's fragile ear. Walker would already know what that meant; no fun explaining to him. "It will not only turn your lovely house into dust, it will separate every part of you from every other part of you."

Senator McComb allowed his lips to brush the side of her delicate neck. Too bad there wasn't more time . . .

He smiled at that.

Walker raised his bloody face.

"Let her go," he panted. "You've got me."

Begging was always nice, but moments were now short. McComb shrugged.

"You're not the one I want. 'Agent' Walker is too visible, sad to say. But 'Officer' Walker dead is just another D.C. statistic, and when he's gone, so are *you*."

He looked over at Cole. "Go get the other one. I want him to see this."

Cole frowned stupidly. "He's dead—"

McComb sighed. Unfortunate that Cole was such a moron. "If he were dead, you *jerk,* this one wouldn't be here!"

Cole turned and went toward the front of the house, mumbling to himself. McComb shrugged to Reyes and then grinned again, happily watched their lives tick away toward nothingness . . .

It seemed to take hours to make his way to the side of the house, and Max thanked God for bulletproof vests with every dragging inch. Consciousness swam in and out of his pain-fogged sight, blended with the darkness. He didn't have a plan, but they were in the kitchen, he knew that much—even from his crawl through the swamp of his muddy yard, he could see the light that shimmered across the lawn from the back of the house—

Max didn't see the shotgun until he was on top of it. The ache in his chest was incredible, obliterated all else—

—except the thoughts of Melissa and the baby.

He picked up the dripping weapon, then looked over at the dead man who lay in the muck, winced at the gore that was flecked across his splayed thighs. Water had collected in pools on top of the man's open eyes, magnifying them. Diluted blood ran over his chin.

You look like I feel.

He worked the pump's action. Empty. He searched the man's pockets with shaking hands. Found a shell, then another, a third. He loaded the twelve-gauge and then used the butt of it as a crutch, raised himself up, and stumbled toward the back porch.

He stopped at the kitchen window and peered through the fragmented glass.

Four people. Two men, one cuffed, head down, the other with a pistol in hand.

And *'Lissa,* held firmly by another man—

He moved closer, aimed at the stranger who gripped his wife. Then blinked the rain out of his eyes and shook his head slightly. The man looked familiar, but he couldn't place him—familiar, but *wrong* somehow . . .

Didn't matter if it was the Devil Himself. *"Let her go!"* he screamed, shotgun raised unsteadily.

They all jerked toward the window, and the man with the pistol raised it to fire at him.

Max squeezed the trigger, and half of the stranger's head blew across the kitchen before he got completely turned around.

That's when it hit him; the man who held his wife was *Senator* Aaron McComb—

Or McComb's father—

The politician dove for cover, took Melissa with him.

Another man, the one who had shot him at the upstairs window, ran into the kitchen, a heavy pistol, .45, pointed at the glass.

Walker raised the shotgun and blew a second shot across the ceiling. The kitchen light exploded, and the room was plunged into darkness.

The killer with the gun returned fire, but his aim was wild. Walker saw the cuffed man, a hulking shadow, drop easily to the floor, and the silhouettes of his young wife and Senator McComb.

He saw movement. Was that somebody else?

Somebody who stumbled out of the kitchen, toward the living room?

A flash of movement. He aimed as best he could in the dark and discharged the last round into the shadows—

And hit the wall, blew the flowered wallpaper into shreds.

He had missed.

He jacked the slide, clicked on empty. He dropped the shotgun.

The killer heard the firing pin hit air. He laughed brutally, a sharp, grating sound, and rushed out onto the back porch.

Max stumbled away, but he was hurting too bad to get far.

The killer in the long coat strode across the yard, holstered his gun, and kicked Max in the belly without slowing down.

He doubled over, and the grinning man kneed him in the face.

He felt hot blood squirt from his nose. He went down, barely aware that the man kicked at his shattered ribs, again and again.

The burst of pain lowered to a screaming ache. He rolled over onto his back and looked up at the killer, dazed and bloody.

"What—do you want?"

The killer pulled his gun and cocked it, pointed it smoothly at Walker's face. He dropped to his knees so Walker could hear him better—

"You're a bright boy . . . why don't you sleep on it?"

Walker stared into the blackness of the bore—

—*Oh, 'Lissa. I'm sorry*—

—and tensed for the end.

". . . why don't you sleep on it?"

Walker stepped forward, hands free from the cuffs; the keys had been on the man with half a head.

"I already did that," he said. Rain smoothed his fevered head.

His younger self was barely conscious, but he raised his battered face to the sound of his own voice.

Cole spun, eyes wide. He knew, but hadn't seen yet. For a split second he froze, caught in the TEC man's icy gaze.

It was long enough.

Walker kicked the gun out of Cole's hand with a snap of his right foot and sprang into him.

He was driven by ten years of pain, and all of the fantasies he'd had, played over and over in his mind until he thought he'd go insane. Ten years of rage. A decade of anger—

He slammed both fists into Cole's ribs, smashed the bones.

He drove his elbow into the ugly, cruel face, broke the nose, felt it shatter—

Cole staggered, but he was trained. He feinted, dropped back, then kicked Walker's bruised gut.

Walker groaned, but the fury kept him on his feet. He tackled Cole and they fell and rolled in the mud, driving blows into each other with machine-like efficiency. The pain didn't matter.

Walker's hate fucked him up. He was so intent on killing, he missed Cole's knee as it came up—

And rammed high into his torso, hit the solar plexus, knocked the air out of him. He . . . couldn't . . . breathe . . .

Cole came up, jerked Walker with him, and held onto his shoulders, tight. He kicked and kneed brutally, over and over—

Cole had him, and they both knew it. He had been through too much to stand any more, and Cole was going to kill him.

"Your wife's gonna *beg* me to finish her!" Cole screamed into his face, and brought his leg back to end it.

—NO—!

Fresh rage surged through him. It wasn't a cure but it was enough. The pain fled into a dark corner of his mind, and he blocked the kick with an arm made out of steel.

He lunged forward, his whole being bent on living long enough to see this man destroyed. Each step became the beginning of a kick into Cole's body, each step one more closer to being able to smash Cole's face into a bloody pulp.

—Bad mistake, you fuck—

Cole blubbered with pain and fear as Walker kicked the shit out of him, drove him through the mud and rain to slam against the side of the house.

He was almost used up when he threw the final kick, the one that would smash the bastard's fucking skull in, and Cole, in a desperate block, caught it.

Beyond conscious thought, Walker used it. He jumped into the air and over his own leg with the other foot. Cole's neck was trapped in between, a scissor lock—

Walker flipped him to the ground, relished the thick snap as the killer's spine cracked.

Cole twitched and spasmed, eerily silent, choked on the aspirated blood—

And died.

Walker smiled through his pain and then turned to look at the young cop with his face.

Max stared up at his older twin through a wet crimson mask, obviously convinced that he was hallucinating . . .

He remembered it, now. He met his younger gaze and spoke clearly.

"Stay out of this," he said, then turned and ran back to the house. "I'll get her."

This was his fight and he was ten years wiser.

He stopped in the shattered kitchen and found Handcuff's gun, scooped it up, started for the second floor.

He hurried up the stairs, pain put aside. Movement on the landing, sounds of a struggle. Walker crept up the last few steps, weapon raised—

McComb and 'Lissa—there *was* no one else.

McComb threw her against a landing window, her face pressed to the glass, then jerked her back.

McComb had heard him come up. The aging senator turned, smiled cruelly, maniacally—

· · ·

Max felt as if he were dying, but maybe it wasn't that bad—

Nothing mattered but Melissa—her and their baby. The old stranger was his ally, their friend—

—*He's me*—

No, it couldn't be.

Max raised his bloody head and saw Melissa's face framed in an upstairs window, just for an instant. Her wan features were stretched into agony, for him—

"'Lissa," he whispered, and tried to raise a hand, reach her, but the rain was in his way, and suddenly she was jerked out of sight.

He had to get to her.

He knew he couldn't make it in time.

If there *was* a God—or even a stranger with his face—

—*Save her!*

·

Twenty-Four

McComb felt more powerful than he ever had before as he held the gun to Melissa Walker's head, a bigger high than with Parker. Perhaps it was because she was so beautiful, so delicate—

Or perhaps it was because he was going to destroy her in front of her husband—and he wasn't going to be able to do a thing about it.

Rain crashed to the floor from a shattered window behind them. Walker rose into view, climbed the stairs slowly.

The rest of his men were dead, McComb was sure—the TEC agent looked like shit, muddy and battered. And if he was still walking, Cole wasn't—no great loss.

McComb pressed the barrel into her temple firmly; Mrs. Walker didn't move a centimeter . . .

"It's different than before, isn't it?" McComb spoke as gently as possible over the rain, smiled at Walker. "That's what happens when you change time. Lines of confluence, probability scales, all that shit."

Walker still held his gun, kept it pointed down. McComb raised his eyebrows.

Really, and him an agent . . .

"Put the gun on the floor," he said tiredly. "What are you going to do, *shoot* me?"

Walker let the gun slide to the carpet and his wide shoulders slumped, almost imperceptibly. McComb smiled again; would the man ever learn *anything*?

"There's a bomb about to go off any second now," he said easily. "You know what happens then? We're all dead, and I win by default! My young self is still going to be President." He squeezed Melissa closer.

"And you can't save your wife, just like you couldn't before."

Walker's eyes sparked fire, but he didn't move. "She died because you came back and made changes."

Oh, the irony! "And so now *you're* fucking with time, which makes you as bad as me . . ."

Walker's scarred face was the epitome of self-righteousness. "Wrong. I'm setting it right."

Sure, whatever. "I don't think so. You know, I hate having to do things over again—except in this case"—McComb shrugged helplessly—"I don't see any other option . . ."

Walker's voice was suddenly firmer, colder. "I do."

The battle-scarred agent had his head cocked to one side, and McComb frowned, kept the pistol steady on Walker. And then he heard the footsteps—

The young Senator McComb stepped onto the landing.

McComb felt a hot flash of panic, then stomped on it. This wasn't supposed to happen, this *couldn't* happen—

"What are you *doing* here?!"

The young senator's face pinched into an expression of irritated confusion. "Who're you yelling at? You called me. I got the message from the Senate operator . . ."

McComb felt it sink in as he glared at the younger man. *The bomb!*

"I didn't leave any message, you fucking *idiot*!"

Walker smiled, a little twitch at the corners of his mouth. "Don't argue among yourself . . . I left it." His smile widened. "And now *nobody's* got a future."

McComb stared at the agent, felt sweat suddenly ooze from every pore in his body. He kept the gun raised, glanced down at the C4—

Thirty-five seconds.

. . . Thirty-five seconds until the end of his life, his career, his future.

All thanks to Max Walker.

Walker looked at Melissa, caught her gaze. He flicked his own downward, motioned for her to watch his hand . . .

Three fingers out. 'Lissa got it, nodded with her chin.

The old McComb glared at him angrily, his weasely features twisted into frustrated hate. "Look at this mess. You turned an ordinary murder into a *bloodbath*! It could've just been you, Walker!"

Walker dropped to two fingers, then one.

The older senator looked away, screamed into the panicked young McComb's face. "Get out of here! Go, *now*!"

Walker tensed, retracted his last finger—

Melissa lashed out, brought her elbow around and caught the old McComb in the side of the nose. He stumbled back, jerked the trigger—

Walker saw 'Lis take the bullet through the back of her shoulder. It ripped through her flesh. Blood immediately seeped through, surrounded the wound with a widening aura of red.

A split second. Walker reached and grabbed the young McComb, threw him at his older image.

The McCombs were now a half meter apart. "You two should be closer," said Walker.

"Get him away from me! Get him away!" The old senator shrank back as if the youth were a particularly horrible spider.

Walker felt nothing but ice in his heart. "Same matter can't occupy the same space . . ."

He smiled at the old McComb. And found that he couldn't resist a parting shot. "You know, I'm still kicking—I must be on Broadway."

Walker grinned. And kicked the young senator in the back.

"No—!"

Time halted. As the two images touched, they began to burn with a blinding phosphorescent energy, but for all the light, there was no heat. It was a cold fire, but a deadly one. Their heads fell back in unison, mouths opened. They screamed in silence, the only sound a heavy electric hum. As though the air around them expanded into noise.

Their arms joined, overlapped. Limbs twisted together, glowed with a brilliant light. Within a few seconds, there were no longer two distinct images, no humanity to the creation—

The taffy-like monster writhed in agony. Their—its—screams drowned out the strange hum—monstrous bellowings of pain and terror, no longer Aaron McComb.

Time stumbled onward . . .

The monster reeled around, toward the broken second-story window, dragged tracers of sparking air behind it.

Walker turned and looked at Melissa. Her shoulder wasn't too bad; she was going to be okay. They had maybe five seconds—

"Max," she whispered, and the sweetness there gave him the strength he was going to need.

"It's not my time yet," he said gently, and found that the thought brought no pain. Doing what he meant to do . . .

it could kill him, or perhaps he'd just disappear forever. But he saw in her loving eyes that she understood, and it was all he needed to know.

Walker tensed, then ran at the McComb creature, arms spread. He slammed into it, felt the burning energy—

They crashed out the window, and as they tumbled down the roof, Walker saw the vortex come for them. Time bent and shimmered, reflected in the shiny pools of rain. The energy expanded, cradled them as they plunged off the edge and toward the ground—

The bomb exploded, but into the vortex. It was beautiful; Walker saw the glow around them spread electric fingers across the sky, and he realized the pain had fled. Fragments of light, shrapnel, blew a warm wind through his hair—

—and they were gone.

The light and sound were overpowering. Max closed his beaten eyelids against the worst of it, but he was nearly blinded anyway.

And then as quickly as it had come, the event was over. The rain had finally slacked off; it drizzled lightly now across his aching skin. He dragged himself up, not sure if he had passed out, dreamed the glowing men—

Must've dreamed it; had to. He wasn't sure *what* had happened, really, not any of it—

"'*Lis.*'" His voice was a rusty croak.

He struggled to the front door, nearly collapsed more than once; the thought of her urged him on.

He climbed the stairs, every step an agony—but nothing compared to what he felt when he saw her on the landing.

Blood everywhere, staining the front of her robe with crimson flowers.

He ran or fell to her side, reached out to stroke her matted hair, heart dying inside of him. God, why hadn't they just killed him? Why—

Melissa opened her eyes and looked up at him. ". . . Max?"

The tears spilled out now, but he suddenly wanted to laugh, scream with joy. "I'm here," he whispered harshly, and started to cry harder.

"Oh, God, 'Lissa, I thought I'd—thought I lost you . . ." He wrapped his leaden arms around her gently, softly, and rocked back and forth.

"Not again." Her voice was strong, but her fingers were gentle; they came up to caress his wet hair, the back of his neck.

Max cried because he didn't understand what had happened, but his heart sang with love; it was over, and they were still alive. Still together.

They held each other for a long, long time.

Twenty-Five

Walker kept his eyes closed through the jump, prepared to face the blankness. Melissa was alive, and if that meant his own life was over, fine. He could die with that.

He felt the vortex spin, heard the McComb creature scream, felt it pull away from him in the absence of physical movement—felt it dissipate into the void . . .

The no-time suddenly crashed into sound and motion. He was restrained, rushed through the blankness. And then screeched to a halt.

The reverberations of the explosion died away in his mind as he opened his eyes—

He sat in a TEC launch pod, alone. Walker opened his eyes wider and looked around, incredulous—

No mud, no water, no pain. His uniform was clean.

Walker caught a glimpse of himself in a mirrored surface on the console. His face was clean, free of cuts and bruises . . .

He peered closer. Something else was different, too, though he couldn't place it.

He popped the restraints and hopped out onto the deck.

Several techs smiled and nodded at him, friendlier than he remembered them . . .

He acted normal, got out of the pod and signed the paperwork. His body felt strong, healthy, and the launch room looked comfortably familiar, nothing disassembled—

What happened? And what had changed?

Stunned, he walked out of the launch room and into the crowded corridor. Techs and other staffers smiled or grinned at him, acted happy to see him—but he had no real friends, not since 'Lissa had died . . .

It was like a dream. A bizarre unreality.

He headed by habit to the squad room, and stopped dead in front of the door, heart in his throat—

Eugene Matuzak stood in the doorway and grinned at him.

Matuzak saw Max Walker headed toward him and smiled. Max still owed him ten bucks from the Bears game. "Where *you* goin', Walker?"

The agent halted and turned wide eyes to Matuzak. His usual tan seemed to blanch, and his jaw dropped open.

"What happened to you?" he said, acting as if Mat had suddenly sprouted wings or something.

"What do you mean?" It sounded like one of Walker's jokes.

"You're walking around."

Mat shook his head, grinned wider. "Yeah, I been doin' that for a while, since I was like a year old; weird, huh?"

Walker looked around the squad room as if he'd never seen it before. Several of the guys waved at him, but Max was being uncharacteristically subdued. He walked over to one of the Datalink computers and touched the logo etched into the side.

Mat stepped closer to see what Max looked at: "Parker

196

Datalink Systems" and the picture of the wave. Nothing strange about that . . .

The man was definitely not himself. Matuzak frowned, concerned. He had been okay this morning, wisecracking like always . . .

The agent turned and asked casually, "So, what's going on with that senator? McComb?"

Matuzak looked at him skeptically. "*Aaron* McComb?"

He nodded earnestly, and Mat started to laugh, though still a little worried. It was a joke, obviously, but Jesus, what an odd sense of humor!

"You want time off, ask for it, Max. Really, you deserve a few days anyway, and what *is* this shit?" He smiled again, waited for the punch line.

He grinned back, but he seemed uneasy. "I got a blank spot."

Blank spot? "You got a hole in your head. No one's heard anything from him in ten years; he's probably in the twilight zone, playing cards with Hoffa."

Matuzak studied Walker closely; *he* knew that. Long day, maybe—'cause there was definitely something that he was missing on this one—

"Right," said Max, and then smiled easily. "I remember. Too bad, eh?"

"You okay?" Mat cocked an eyebrow at his old friend. "Jump went okay?"

Walker clapped him on the arm. "Just fine, Mat."

That was more like it. "Then what're you hangin' around here for?"

He shrugged. "Slumming, I guess."

Matuzak waved him off, but Walker turned and looked at him seriously on the way out the door.

"It's good to see you," he said, simple but sincere. His eyes seemed different somehow . . .

Walker nodded at a few of the guys and headed for home. Swerling had caught part of the conversation; he looked over at Mat and rolled his eyes. Walker had stumped all of them with his little tricks at one time or another, an endearing if obnoxious little habit—

Shit, my ten bucks! Yeah, Max was still Max.

Matuzak sighed and headed for the office to call Carol. Maybe they could go out to dinner for a change; she had plans to make her Hungarian stew . . .

Yuck.

Walker headed for the front of the building, still uncertain about everything. Was Melissa alive? She must be, had to be—reality was different now, all of it . . .

As he walked through the corridor to the exit, he found himself grinning happily at the passing faces. They were all familiar to him, but they had never acted as if Walker were a friend, a good guy to know—it was something he hadn't missed in his life before, the camaraderie and friendships of coworkers; now it seemed he had it, like it or not.

He liked it.

As he pushed through the exit into the lobby, he was stopped again—

Sarah Fielding, wearing a light, sexy dress, walked past him. As their eyes met, a small, flirtatious smile flicked across her lips.

Walker smiled back. As they passed, he said, "Stay out of trouble this time, Fielding."

She stopped and looked at him uncertainly. "I'm sorry, do I know you?"

He was amazed, again. This reality, would he get used to it? "I guess not," he said.

She smiled again, then turned to walk away.

He couldn't help himself. "Hey . . . Bobby Trapasso is still waiting for that second chance," he said.

Fielding turned a startled gaze back at him, and he smiled sweetly and walked away, before she could say a word.

He got into his squad car and sat for a moment, absorbed the strangeness of it all. He realized that his hands were shaking; what else was different?

"Home," he said, and the computer targeted and pulled out.

It was a beautiful, sunny day, early afternoon. Light played over the streets, made the air seem clean and sparkly. The city hadn't changed, or at least nothing he could make out—but it was pretty to look at. Flowers bloomed in the trees . . .

The car led him toward his apartment complex—and drove right past it. He felt nothing but relief—except for a tiny flicker of hope. That he didn't live there anymore, that meant—well, it *could* mean . . .

He pushed the thoughts aside, concentrated on the simple pleasure of the passing day. He'd know soon enough.

The city gradually fell away, and the car took him through a series of tree-lined neighborhoods, toward their old house—

He switched to manual as he got closer. His heart started to pound as the car turned the corner, past neighboring houses, into the cul-de-sac where they had once lived. Ten years before . . .

He slammed on the brakes and stared.

Their house, their beautiful home that had been destroyed in 1994, sat behind the lush grass of the front yard, freshly painted. The trees on either side glittered with budding young leaves, light green against the blue sky.

And a boy of about eight or nine with hair the color of

Walker's stood on the lawn. When the child saw Walker's car, he raised one slender arm and waved.

Walker couldn't hear, but the boy's smiling mouth formed the words clearly, and Walker felt the last of the hardness around his heart slip away; there was no room for it anymore.

The boy, whose name he didn't even know, had called out to someone in the house.

Dad's home—!

Yes.

Dad's home.

Max Walker laughed out loud and went to greet his wife and son.

Epilogue

Melissa Walker smiled to herself as she sliced potatoes, dropped the pieces into the pot of water. Potato salad to go with the barbecue, if Max was in the mood to haul out the grill . . .

She had to remember to call Mom, tonight maybe—no, tomorrow. Tonight was just for her and Max and Tommy. They could spread a blanket out in the backyard, bring some books and magazines out with them. Tommy was thrilled with the telescope they'd given him for his birthday; after dark, he and Max would stay up too late, watching for meteors . . .

She heard Tommy call out from the front, and her husband's car pull into the driveway.

She grabbed a dish towel from the counter and wiped her hands on it absently as she walked for the front door. She was glad that he'd gotten off early; the timing was perfect . . .

She looked out the window in time to see Max get out of his car and beckon to Tommy; their son ran to him and tackled him with a flying hug that knocked both of them onto the grass. He was such a wonderful father—sometimes her heart was so full when she looked at the two of them together, she—she just could hardly stand it. They had the same hair, same eyes, same beautiful smile; her boys.

She watched Tommy babble up at Max about barbecued hot dogs; Max grinned indulgently, laughed about something.

She opened the front door, excited and nervous. Her smile felt glued on, big as her face.

When Max looked up and saw her, his own face broke into a grin. He stood and walked to her quickly. His arms came up, wrapped around her tightly.

She hugged him back, pleased with the intensity of the embrace, then stepped back to look him over.

"What kind of day did you have?"

He shrugged, still grinning. "Busy . . ."

He moved forward and hugged her again, hands reaching up to stroke her hair.

"Hey, you all right?" He was usually affectionate, but today he seemed almost high on something, giddy.

"I'm *great*," he said, so happily that she laughed.

"Yeah, you *are*," she said playfully.

She draped an arm around his waist and they started for the house. Tommy ran up alongside, and Max reached down and scooped him up easily.

She leaned closer to her husband and whispered gently in his ear.

"I've got something I want to tell you," she said, and smiled, truly happy.

Maybe it would be a girl this time . . .

He leaned over and kissed her gently on the lips. "Take your time," he whispered back. "I'm not going anywhere . . ."

Walker went inside with his family, feeling at peace with it all.

He was finally home.

It was about time.